LOONEY TUNES

BACK

Adapted by Jenn

SCHOLASTIC INC.

New York Toronto London Auckland Sydney
Mexico City New Delhi Hong Kong Buenos Aires

ISBN 0-439-52136-X

Designed by Peter Koblish

12 11 10 9 8 7 6 5 4 3 2   3 4 5 6 7 8/0

Printed in the U.S.A.

First printing, October 2003

1. Act One, Scene One. And . . . Action!

Daffy was disconsolate. Depressed. Also despondent, distraught, and downright dejected. Not to mention discouraged. His acting career was in the doldrums, his popularity dwindling. And now, the know-nothing junior executives at Warner Brothers were shaking their heads and looking doubtful.

He'd just shown them the latest scenes from the blockbuster he was shooting — starring none other than himself, of course — and they didn't seem to *get* it. What was there to get? What could be better than Elmer Fudd as an evil clown, thundering along atop an old-fashioned circus calliope? The only way to top that shot was to have the hero (Daffy, naturally) face off against the steam-spewing, clown-driven, music-playing mechanical monstrosity. The finale? Using his immense intelligence and a sophisticated computer chip, our hero blows the whole pipe organ — and its driver — to smithereens.

1

The enormous fireball exploded, the screen went dark. Then the lights came up in the conference room. Daffy smiled at the execs around the table, and at Mr. Warner and his brother. The smile died on his face when he saw their expressions.

"Wait!" he said desperately. "There's a love story."

Mr. Warner looked perplexed. "You killed Elmer," he said flatly.

"You can't kill Elmer," added Mr. Warner's brother.

Daffy started to babble. "He comes back from the dead later," he said, making it up as he went along. "He's even crazier, with scars on his face and everything."

Elmer, sitting next to Mr. Warner, spoke up nervously. "I don't want to play a cwazy clown. I'm afwaid of clowns."

Daffy rolled his eyes. Could it get any worse?

It could.

Just then, a figure appeared in the doorway.

"What's up, doc?"

It was Bugs. Bugs, the "It" toon. The star of the moment. Everybody's sweetheart. Mr. Box Office. The rabbit's career was sky-high, and he could do no wrong.

The entire roomful of executives cracked up just at the sight of him.

Daffy frowned. Steam leaked from his ears as he watched Bugs stroll into the room, his people bustling around him to make sure he was comfortable and happy. One assistant pulled out his chair while another wiped it with a handkerchief. A personal lighting technician held a spotlight over the rabbit's head, casting Bugs's features in a flattering glow.

Bugs sat down and looked over at Daffy. "So, Daff," he said casually, "I was reading this rewrite you did, and, uh, I only got one question." He paused. "Where's *me*?"

Daffy rolled his eyes. "Actors," he hissed. "I was just getting to *your* part, Bugsy," he said. He nodded to the projectionist, and the screen came to life again. The calliope's metal claw held a confused-looking Bugs high above the city. He was screaming in fear. At that exact moment, the claw released Bugs and he went hurtling toward the street. Until . . . Daffy swooped into the frame and swung Bugs to safety. "My hero!" cried Bugs, swooning.

Then a toilet fell out out of the sky and flattened him.

The screen went dark again and the lights in the room came up. Bugs yawned and got up to go, tossing away the stub of the carrot he'd been snacking on. One of his assistants caught it before it hit the floor, while another handed Bugs a fresh one. "Toilet humor." Bugs said to Daffy. "I'll pass."

Daffy looked disgusted. "Thanks for stopping by. I'm a big fan . . . of your *early* work."

"Excuse me," someone said. It was the pretty young woman who'd been sitting at the other end of the table. "I'm sorry," she said, "but I don't think we can have a Bugs Bunny movie without Bugs Bunny."

Daffy went over to her. "If you don't mind my asking," he said politely, sprinkling her with a sparkling spray of spittle, "whose assistant are you?"

The woman stuck out her hand to shake Daffy's. "Kate Houghton," she said. "Executive Vice President, Comedy." Her eyes were serious, her mouth a thin line.

No sense of humor, but the dame had a good grip. Daffy had to hand it to her.

Mr. Warner spoke up. "Kate did *Lethal Weapon Babies,*" he said, pointing to a poster of Danny Glover and Mel Gibson in diapers. The caption said "Nap Time's Over."

His brother sighed happily. "Finally, a *Lethal Weapon* I can take my grandchildren to."

"We've brought Kate aboard," Mr. Warner explained, "because we think she can really add something to the Looney Tunes mix."

Daffy only had to think for a second before deciding on the best course of action: sucking up to Kate. "Fresh perspective," he sputtered smilingly. "Just what we need! New ideas for a post–Bugs Bunny world."

Kate pulled out her phone/computer and punched a few buttons, bringing up charts and graphs to illustrate what she was saying. "Actually," she informed Daffy, "our latest research shows that Bugs Bunny is a core asset who appeals to male and female, young and old, throughout the known universe . . ."

Bugs was blushing modestly.

". . . while the duck's fan base is limited to angry fat guys in basements," Kate finished. "And there's only seven of them."

"Did you count Ted?" Daffy managed to squeak out.

"Yes," Kate answered.

Nervously, Daffy turned to the brothers. "C'mon," he pleaded. "I'm thrice the entertainer the rabbit is!"

Bugs let out a colossal, rumbling belch. The room rocked with laughter.

Daffy didn't join in. "Yes, he's hilarious," he said sarcastically. "But moviegoers these days demand action!" He went into a kung fu routine, a blur of kicks and flying fists. "Hah!" he cried. "Ho! Ah-cha-cha!" His moves were faster than lightning, but when the smoke had cleared Daffy was left with one arm stuck in his ear, right up to the elbow. Gently, he extracted his hand and shook it off. "Top that, rabbit!"

Gracefully, Bugs twisted himself into a pretzel pose. "Kong Que," he said solemnly. "The Peacock." One leg flicked out and a toe tapped Daffy on the head. Daffy's eyeballs popped out and bounced around on the table.

The execs went wild.

Daffy grabbed his eyeballs and held them up to peer at Bugs. "Despicable," he sputtered into Bugs's face.

"You can't have his eyeballs falling out like that," Kate remarked. "It makes people think of their own eyeballs falling out."

Daffy shoved his eyeballs back in. "So," he said. "It has come to this. I'm afraid the Warner Brothers must choose between a handsome matinee idol" — he puffed out his chest and showed them his profile — "or this miscreant perpetrator of low burlesque." He pointed at Bugs.

The brothers whispered for a moment. "Miscreant perpetrator of low burlesque?" said Mr. Warner.

"Whichever one is not the duck," agreed his brother.

"You're firing Daffy Duck?" Kate asked, astonished.

"I'm not firing Daffy Duck," said Mr. Warner.

"I'm not firing Daffy Duck," said Mr. Warner's brother.

"You're firing Daffy Duck," the brothers told Kate.

Kate looked stunned. "I'm sorry it has come to this." She started to walk Daffy out of the room.

Tears came to Daffy's eyes. "Wait!" he cried. "I haven't tried toadying, kowtowing, or bootlicking yet! Please! Help me! I'm too moist and tender to retire! Please, Brother! Other Brother! Icy she-wolf! Help me!" He clung desperately to Kate's leg.

It was an all-time low for the duck.

2. Holy Tsunami, Batman!

Daffy squirmed like a snake at yoga class, trying to get out of Kate's grip and pleading, "I'll do anything! I'll work with animals! Dogs! Big, smelly, unhouse-broken dogs. I'll play food!" But she marched him out onto the lot and right up to a tall, handsome security guard. Then she handed him over. Bugs came along, watching contentedly as Kate demanded, "Toss this duck off the lot."

"*This* duck?" asked the security guard, whose name tag said D.J. "This is Daffy Duck!"

"Not anymore," Kate said, dusting off her hands. "We own the name." She turned to Bugs and smiled. "How does Snooty's sound for lunch?"

"A little pretentious," Bugs observed.

"Oh yeah?" Daffy said. "You can't stop me from calling myself D—" Stunned, he stopped. "Well, what do you know? I can't say my own name!"

D.J. was filling out a form, writing on his clipboard. "You fired Daffy Duck?" he asked.

"No, I didn't," Kate replied. "Well, I did, they did . . . we did."

"Ah, but you were just following orders, right? Hard on the soul being the Messenger of Death, isn't it?" D.J. said.

Kate's eyes narrowed. "You don't know me."

D.J. stared back at her. "You're Kate Haughton, you're the VP of comedy. Go figure. You drive a red 1988 Alfa Romeo. Good engine. A little under-driven. I know this because you nearly ran me over last week. But why would you care? I'm just a security guard."

"Just eject the duck," Kate replied.

"Can't do that," D.J. said.

"Why not?"

"He's gone."

Kate looked around and spotted Daffy slipping through the crowd of stagehands who were carrying props and scenery back and forth. "Stop!" she cried. She turned to D.J. "Stop him!"

D.J. spoke into his radio to the other security guards. "Boys, it's duck season."

Daffy jumped into the cab of a crane that was hoisting a gigantic stone monkey head high over the lot. Grinning, he pulled a lever and the monkey statue fell, dropping right toward D.J.'s head.

D.J. caught the monkey head in one hand and tossed it over to a stagehand. Fake rock, made of Styrofoam.

Next, Daffy scrambled up a ladder that was propped against the back of a set for a city apartment building. He pulled the ladder up after him and disappeared through a window, just as D.J. caught up with him. D.J. climbed up the side of the building behind Daffy and followed him out the window — only to find himself standing on a narrow ledge, right next to the caped crusader himself.

Batman.

"Cut!" yelled the director from below.

D.J. turned to look, lost his footing, and fell three stories.

Fortunately, there was a giant air bag on the ground.

D.J. bounced a few times. "I'm all right!" he yelled.

"Who cares?" the director yelled back.

Just then, D.J. turned to see Daffy climbing behind the wheel of the Batmobile. "To the Duckcave!" Daffy spluttered, revving the engine of the sleek, black vehicle. It purred like a giant kitten.

D.J. sprinted over and hauled Daffy out of the car. It was time to get this duck off the set! He marched Daffy down the Gotham City "street." Behind them, flames shot out of the back of the Batmobile. D.J. didn't notice.

Daffy did.

"So," said Daffy chattily, "feeling pretty good about yourself?"

"I am," D.J. admitted.

"You bested that dastardly duck," Daffy said, looking over his shoulder to check on the Batmobile, which was now starting to move. It picked up speed quickly, moving faster and faster. Actors and crew members scattered in all directions as the car plowed through the crowd.

"And now you're going to offer your catch to the pretty executive," Daffy went on flattering D.J.

"Indeed," said D.J.

Behind him, the Batmobile crashed into the looming Warner Brothers water tower, taking out one of its major supports.

At that moment, Kate and Bugs cruised by in her convertible, chatting about how *over* Daffy's career was.

"Hey!" D.J. shouted to Kate. He held Daffy up to show off his catch. Behind him, the water tower was toppling over, as if in slow motion. A wall of water spilled out of it.

The legs of the tower missed D.J. and Daffy completely, but the towering wave drenched Kate and Bugs. The car filled up until it looked like a kiddie pool. Bugs stuck on a pair of sunglasses and hopped onto a rowboat, completely dry. "Man," he said, laughing, "he keeps topping himself!"

Kate barely heard him. She was glaring at D.J.

"I think she likes you," Daffy said to D.J.

D.J. didn't answer.

Two seconds later, Daffy and D.J. found themselves flying off the lot. They landed with a thud on the sidewalk. Daffy was pasted to D.J.'s face. D.J. was no longer wearing his security guard uniform.

"Let me get off your face there," Daffy said, peeling himself away. He gestured inside the gates, where chaos reigned as the Batmobile screeched through the lot and water soaked everything. "Guess I better give them a couple hours to cool off. So, where for lunch? I'm banned at the following restaurants: Spago, Musso, Der Wienerschnitzel —"

"Go away," D.J. said, interrupting the duck's chatter. He was busy unlocking a motorbike from a nearby pole.

Daffy looked hurt. "Hey, what gives? We've shared."

"And it was a delight," D.J. said. "But now I must move on with my life, which, it saddens me to report, will not include any insane ducks."

Daffy drew himself up. "Fine," he sputtered. "Sayonara, Superstar! Pasta la vista!"

D.J. paid no attention to the duck's ranting. He

climbed onto the bike, started it up, and took off in a cloud of dust.

Daffy coughed. A security guard stuck his head through the gate and yelled, "Duck!"

"Oh, yes!" Daffy cried. "They've seen the error of their ways and want me back! Coming! No apologies necessary! Everyone makes stupid mistakes!"

The security guard placed Daffy's suitcase on the ground and walked away. Daffy sighed, tried to pick it up, and eventually just left it there.

Meanwhile, Kate and Bugs had settled on the studio commissary for lunch. The place was full of stars: Shaggy, Scooby, and Matthew Lillard sat at the next table, arguing over Matthew's interpretation of Shaggy in the live-action movie.

Kate seemed preoccupied. "Don't worry," Bugs told her. "Daffy always comes back. I just tell him how much I need him. We hug. We cry. I drop something heavy on him. I laugh."

Kate shrugged, making a few notes on her phone/computer. "The duck's gone," she said. "He's history." She crossed something out. "He's deleted."

"You'll go far in this business," Bugs said admiringly.

"I already have," said Kate, snapping her phone shut. "The question is, how can I help *you*? Answer: team you up with a hot female costar."

Bugs considered this. "I don't think I'd feel right about dropping heavy things on a girl," he said.

"We can change the dynamic." Kate was excited, full of ideas. "You still can't stand each other, but *now* you'll fall madly in love."

Bugs balked. "Usually *I* play the female love interest," he said, whipping on a slinky red gown and a flashy platinum-blonde wig.

Kate frowned as Bugs made kissy-faces at her. "Look," she said, "about the cross-dressing thing . . . In the past, funny. Today, disturbing. I'm trying to be nice, but I was brought in to leverage your synergy and I'm not going to let you or some wacky duck —"

"Daffy," Bugs corrected her.

"Wacky, Daffy, Nutty, Fruitcake Duck, whatever," Kate said. "As the executive on this project, I have to insist that we do every single thing I say."

Bugs pulled out five golden statuettes and placed them on the table. "And as the recipient of these," he said, grunting as he hauled his Hollywood Star (jackhammered out of the sidewalk) onto the table next to them, "I insist we do things like we've always done them, which includes getting Daffy back."

The Oscar statuettes began to cheer, "We want Daffy! Bring him back!"

Kate rolled her eyes.

13

3. Drake. Damian Drake.

D.J. pulled up to a huge mansion and cut the engine of his bike. He waved hello to his sweet, elderly neighbor, Granny, and she waved back. Her little yellow bird, Tweety, sat in a cage watching as Granny clipped her hedge. Granny's big black cat, Sylvester, watched Tweety. He should have been watching his tail: Granny snipped it right off by mistake.

When he got inside, D.J. put down his gym bag, shut the door, and sighed. *Zzzzip!* The bag zipped open and Daffy climbed out. "Guess who? Did you miss me?" he asked cheerfully, ignoring the horrified look on D.J.'s face.

"Hey, how —" D.J. could hardly believe his eyes.

"I showed them. In a few days, they'll be kissing my befeathered rump. Begging me to come back. But I won't." Daffy started to walk around, checking out D.J.'s house.

"I'm sorry," D.J. said. "Did I miss the part where I invited you in?"

Daffy was looking at a stack of magazines on the coffee table. Every single one had Bugs on the cover. He snorted.

D.J. looked annoyed. "Perhaps I was being too polite," he said. "Get out!"

Daffy didn't seem to hear. He was reaching into a big aquarium full of brightly colored tropical fish. He grabbed a fluttery-finned blue one and popped it in his mouth.

D.J. grabbed Daffy by the neck, stuck his hand down Daffy's throat, and pulled out the fish, tossing it back into the aquarium. By the time he looked up again, Daffy was about to wreck a crystal vase. *Whap!* D.J. put his hand on top of Daffy's head and squashed him into a demi-Daffy, half his regular size.

"Problem?" Daffy squawked.

"Leave my father's house, now." D.J.'s voice was stern.

Suddenly, Daffy sprang back to normal size. "You live with your *daddy*?" he said, laughing hysterically. Then he caught sight of a framed poster on the wall. His laughter died. He ran over to check out the slick illustration of a handsome spy. *Ice Spies* was the name of the movie. There were also posters for *To Live Instead of Die* and *Scar Causer.* Plastered in mega-movie-star-sized type on every poster was the name Damian Drake. "Oh, my grease and gravy!" sputtered Daffy. "Your dad's Damian Drake, the superspy?"

D.J. sighed. "He's an actor," he corrected Daffy. "He *plays* a spy."

Daffy nodded wisely. "An actor who *plays* a superspy as a cover for *being* a superspy *playing* an actor!" he said.

"You spend a lot of time on the Internet, don't you?" D.J. asked tiredly.

Daffy was too excited to answer. "I'll bet this whole dump's a superspy lair!" he exclaimed. "Nothing is as it seems. You know, you're probably protected by an invisible force field right this minute!" He picked up an apple, threw it, and watched as it hit D.J. in the head. D.J. yelped.

"Ah ha! The force field penetrating apple!" Daffy proclaimed.

His triumph was interrupted by a repeated jingling. D.J. reached for the phone. "Feel free to continue your delusional ranting while I answer my —" The phone was quiet. He looked over at the coffee table. The TV remote was ringing.

Bewildered, D.J. picked up the remote and pushed a button. Across the room, a framed painting morphed into a blank screen. Then an image appeared: Damian Drake himself. The man was suave, smooth, and well-groomed as ever, and he was looking straight back into D.J.'s eyes. "Son?" said the image.

D.J. blinked. "Dad, why are you in the painting?"

"Listen, D.J., I wanted to keep you out of this," said the Damian-image. "But there's no one else I can trust. Oops. Can you hold on a second?" Damian turned away from the camera to punch out an approaching attacker.

D.J.'s jaw dropped. "Are you shooting a movie or something?"

Damian ignored the question. "Come to Las Vegas," he said. He punched another bad guy. "Ask Dusty Tails about the Blue Monkey."

By now, Daffy had joined D.J. He settled himself in for the show, holding a bushel basket of popcorn and a supersized soda. He sipped noisily.

"The Blue Monkey?" D.J. asked.

"It's a diamond," explained his father.

At that, Daffy's eyes grew to ten times their size and started to spin around.

Damian tried to say something else, but he was interrupted by more attackers. "I love you, son," he said finally, as the screen scrolled back up.

Daffy couldn't sit still. He bounced all over the room, babbling, "Diamond? I'm rich! Filthily so! I've joined the leisure class!"

D.J. barely noticed the duck's antics. "I gotta go save my dad," he said, walking out of the room.

Daffy was right by his side. "Yeah, count me in! A spy caper, double agents, exploding bikinis, tigers hanging from helicopters . . . I'm through with showbiz! From now on, I'm going to live the adventure!" he went on. "Okay, first stop, Vegas. Should we jet or copter in?"

"I was just going to take my dad's old car," D.J. told him.

"A spy car?" Daffy grinned. "Let's roll!" But his excitement died when they walked into the garage. Damian Drake's car was a 1974 Gremlin, its boxy yellow body spotted with rust.

"This isn't a spy car. I used to deliver pizzas in this car," said D.J., patting it fondly as he climbed behind the wheel.

Daffy jumped in, too. "*Secret* pizzas? A spy pie, maybe?"

D.J. grabbed the duck and threw him out the window as he backed the car out of the garage. Then he puttered off down the street. Within seconds, Daffy popped up in the backseat and met D.J.'s eyes in the mirror. "You know how I know it's a spy car?" he asked happily. "Because it doesn't *look* like a spy car."

The Gremlin rolled slowly along. Back at the Drake house, the garage door dropped down just as the floor inside flipped over. There in the garage, polished and ready to roll, was the sleek, gleaming silver spy car of Daffy's dreams.

Daffy jumped into the Gremlin's front seat, grabbed D.J.'s cell phone, and punched in a number.

"Eh, what's up, doc?" Bugs answered, yawning. He was sitting backstage at *The Tonight Show*, chatting with a beautiful girl.

"Ha!" Daffy shouted into the phone.

"Daffy?" Bugs asked.

"Just a friendly call," Daffy spluttered smugly, "to tell you what you can do with your precious Hollywood dreams. For, as it so happens, while you're *pretending* to star in an action movie, I'm starring in my own action reality! Me and my sidekick, D.J., are on our way to Vegas to score the Blue Monkey, a king-sized diamond, which, I might add, will enable me to buy my own movie studio, where I will thereafter write, produce, and direct Daffy Duck–filled, Bugs Bunny–free entertainment, for which I believe the public is clamoring!" He stopped to take a breath.

"Daff, listen," Bugs began. Trying to sound sincere, he recited the speech he'd practiced. "We've had our differences, but you're my partner and I need you."

"Ha!" cried Daffy. "Do you hear my laugher? Ha! I repeat, for your delectation: Ha!" He hung up triumphantly.

D.J. reached over and tossed him out the window again.

4. Meanwhile . . .

In the ultra high-tech communications room in the top floor of the looming skyscraper that was Acme headquarters, an imposing figure sat staring at a bank of monitors. Mr. Smith, a colossus of a man, peered at the flickering waveform that pinpointed a particular location in Beverly Hills. Daffy's boasting words emerged from the speakers: "Me and my sidekick, D.J., are on our way to Vegas to score the Blue Monkey." Mr. Smith nodded his humongous head and reached over to switch off the monitors. He was due at a board meeting.

He lumbered down the hall, past rooms where various Acme products and devices were being tested, and into the boardroom, where he took his usual seat. At the head of the table sat the eternally evil Mr. Chairman, stroking a baby crocodile. The crocodile stared at Mr. Smith with hooded eyes, then smiled, showing its sharp white teeth.

Mr. Chairman reached into a mesh cage and pulled

out an insect, which he dropped into the crocodile's mouth. *Gulp!* It was gone.

"Next order of business?" asked Mr. Chairman. Mr. Smith leaned over and whispered something into Mr. Chairman's ear.

"Thank you, Mr. Smith." Mr. Chairman turned to the board. "Grave news, my friends." He reached out a hand to the touch-sensitive controls on the desk in front of him, and a holographic image appeared: D.J.'s Gremlin, trundling down Highway 15! "It appears that Damian Drake's son knows about the Blue Monkey and is on his way to Las Vegas." He dropped another insect into the crocodile's gaping mouth. "He must not learn the location of the diamond before we do." He leaned forward to manipulate the touch pad again. A new image appeared: a nearly empty room. The only object in sight was Damian Drake, strapped into a folding chair. Two men walked into the picture. "How's the interrogation coming?" Mr. Chairman asked the men.

Damian struck out at both men with his feet and they fell to the ground.

"He's about to crack," one of them reported, after scraping himself back to a standing position. Meanwhile, in the background, Damian head-butted the other man.

Mr. Chairman made a disgusted noise and clicked back to the image of the Gremlin. Speaking softly, but with great intensity, he said, "We *cannot* let the good guys win this time, people. We must capture this son of a spy, we must find out the location of the diamond, and we must use its powers for our own diabolical ends!" He cackled, rubbing his hands together. Then he turned to Mr. Smith, all business. "Copy that to all department heads," he added. He petted his crocodile. With a thin smile, he proclaimed, "Soon the Acme Corporation shall tower over all of creation!" He cackled again.

"All of creation!" echoed the board members in unison, adding their evil laughter to Mr. Chairman's.

"But what about the duck?" asked one of the vice presidents suddenly.

Mr. Chairman turned to smile at the man.

"Extra crispy," he said.

5. And Yet Again, Meanwhile . . .

On the set at Warner Brothers, the cast was watching dailies. *Back in Action* was going to be the blockbuster to beat all blockbusters, the action film that would make Bugs the biggest box-office draw in the history of the known universe. The scene they'd shot the day before was a major one. The actors now watched themselves on screen.

"Duck season!"onscreen Bugs was saying.

"Rabbit season!" answered a fake Daffy-voice. It was the fat guy dressed in a duck suit.

Elmer Fudd stood between them, his shotgun at his side. He looked even more bewildered than usual.

"Duck season!" Bugs said again.

"Rabbit season," said the pseudo-Daffy.

"Rabbit season," Bugs said quickly.

"I say it's duck season, and I say fire!" cried the duck-suited guy.

Obediently, Elmer raised his shotgun and aimed at the imitation bird.

Pow! Feathers flew. The screen went dark. The duck was dead. There were groans as the lights came up.

"Guess we probably shoulda filmed that scene last insteada first," remarked Bugs. He sipped on a carrot juice.

"We need another duck," said Mr. Warner.

Kate suggested an aging star. Bugs vetoed the suggestion.

"Well, then," said Mr. Warner, "I'm out of ideas."

"Let's see," Bugs said, tapping his chin thoughtfully. "We need a duck who can take a shotgun blast to the head. Who could it be? Let me think. Hmmm . . ." He stared meaningfully at Kate.

"What do you want me to say?" she asked defensively. "That I got rid of Daffy? Okay. I got rid of Daffy. And I stand by my decision."

Mr. Warner turned to her. "You're fired," he said casually.

"What?" Kate was stunned.

"You got rid of our best duck," explained Mr. Warner's brother.

"You can't fire me!" Kate protested. "My movies have made nine hundred and fifty million dollars!"

"That's not a billion," Mr. Warner reminded her.

Kate's face changed. She was desperate. "I think we

can all agree that the decision to get rid of Daffy was a poor one," she admitted. "But it's time to move on, and by move on I mean reversing course and getting Daffy back."

Mr. Warner nodded approvingly. "By Monday," he added. "This movie is costing the studio a million dollars a day."

Kate made a promise. "I'll have Daffy back by Monday," she vowed.

Right after the meeting, she headed over to D.J.'s house to see if he knew where Daffy was. She searched the whole place, room by room.

D.J. wasn't there.

Bugs was. He popped up everywhere that Kate looked. She did her best to ignore the rascally rabbit.

Finally, Kate spotted the movie posters featuring Damian Drake. That was the last straw. She broke down crying. "I fired the son of our biggest star! This has really been a career-making day, Kate," she told herself as she sobbed. "First, you get rid of that duck everybody hates but then of course they all want him back, but worst of all you insult Bugs Bunny, who you revere and who you've tried to model your life after."

Next to Kate was a suit of armor. The visor lifted. There was Bugs, also weeping. "I hate to see a grown man cry," he sobbed, "especially when it's a girl. Listen, would it make you stop the water works if I told you Daffy said he was going to Las Vegas with that guy, D.J.?"

Kate perked up. Then she frowned. "It might."

"Hey, hey," Bugs said, climbing out of the suit of armor. "Then this oughta make you delirious!" He led her over to a doorway, flicked on a switch, and opened the door. There was the spy car in all its glory. The machine looked fast even when it was sitting still! "How about we travel in style?"

Kate grinned, her tears gone. "Perfect!" she said.

She and Bugs jumped into the car. Kate fastened her seat belt. Bugs fastened his. Then he added a shoulder belt, and another lap belt, and three more belts crisscrossing his body, until he looked like a mummy wrapped in seat belts. He topped off the outfit with a bicycle helmet. Then he turned to Kate. "Las Vegas, driver!" he said grandly.

The car came to life. Dials lit up and the engine rumbled. "Taking you to Las Vegas," said a female voice from the dashboard. With that, the car leapt out of the garage, scaring Grandma, Sylvester, and Tweety half to death. Then it roared down the street, its tires barely touching the pavement.

6. Las Vegas, Here We Come!

D.J. drove the Gremlin as fast as he dared, gripping the steering wheel. Suddenly, Daffy came squeezing through an air vent on the passenger side. He popped back to full size and settled happily in the passenger seat. He smiled at D.J.

"I'm getting a little tired of throwing you out of the car," D.J. told him.

"That's my plan in a nutshell," Daffy admitted.

"But listen up," D.J. said, realizing he was stuck with the duck. "My dad's never asked for help before, and I'm not going to let anything get in my way. So let's not mess up."

Daffy looked offended. "Fine," he said. "And if we run into anything that requires superspy skills," he spluttered, "like cracking wise or smooching dames, you'd better leave that to me. However, if we have any security guarding needs . . ." he began.

D.J. cut him off. "Funny, duck," he said. "But I'm not a security guard, okay? I'm really a stuntman."

"You?" Daffy asked, amazed. He shook his head. "You'd better leave everything to me."

"Duck," D.J. said patiently, "I'd like to remind you that you are a duck. While I am a man! With a man's brain. And opposable thumbs." He held one up, wiggling it in Daffy's face.

"Yeah, but can you do this?" Daffy asked. He reached out, and a gigantic mallet appeared in his hand. He pounded himself on the head until he broke into pieces. The pieces morphed into a whole crowd of tiny little Daffys. They scrambled all over the car, hooting happily. Then they all came together and turned back into Daffy.

Daffy grinned triumphantly.

D.J. just looked at him. "I can grow a beard," he said. Then, changing the subject, he pointed to a sign. "Las Vegas, three miles!" he read.

At that very moment, Mr. Smith strode into the Las Vegas offices of the Wooden Nickel casino. Outside was a blinking neon sign featuring a humongous gun-totin', ten-gallon-hat-wearin' Yosemite Sam. The cartoon cowboy was waving two big neon bags stuffed full of neon gold. The marquee beneath the sign said Welcome to the Wooden Nickel, an Acme Casino. Now Appearing: Dusty Tails!

In the office, Yosemite Sam himself was nodding as he spoke to Mr. Smith. "You want the varmints and what they came for," he said. "I gotcha. But what's in it for me?"

Mr. Smith picked up a treasure chest and hefted it onto Sam's desk. He opened the lid, and a golden glow lit up Sam's greedy face.

An hour later, D.J. and Daffy walked into the Wooden Nickel, looking around in amazement. They were in Las Vegas! The strip outside was crowded and brilliant with neon. And inside the casino was even better. Just as they arrived, a rootin' tootin' cowboy show was going on, featuring a barroom brawl with cartoon cowboys flying in every direction.

Pow! Blam! Suddenly, cartoon bullets were flying through the air. Three of them hit Daffy right in the bill, spinning it around in three different directions. The audience applauded, thinking it was part of the show.

"Wow," said D.J., joining in the applause. "You can almost smell the gunpowder."

"Yes," Daffy answered drily as he adjusted his bill, "an incredible simulation."

* * *

29

Back near the bar, Nasty Canasta and Cottontail Smith stood with their guns smoking. Yosemite Sam smacked his colleagues with his big floppy cowboy hat. "No, you imbeciles!" he shouted, jumping up and down in a rage. "We wait until he gets what he's coming for!"

"*Then* we blast 'em?" asked Nasty Canasta.

"*Then* we blast 'em," Sam agreed.

"Long as we get to blast 'em," Nasty Canasta said, putting his pistol back into its holster.

Clueless, Daffy and D.J. strolled into the casino's theater area, where Dusty Tails would be appearing. They needed to talk to her to find out more about the Blue Monkey. Daffy was looking over a program with her picture on the cover. "Did you know that Dusty Tails sang the theme songs to six Damian Drake movies?" he asked, as D.J. found his way backstage.

D.J. nodded. "Yes," he said. "He's my father. Remember?"

"Your dad's Damian Drake?" said Daffy.

"Yes!" DJ spat.

"I'm kidding — relax!" Daffy replied. "We did that, okay?" He turned to the stage. "Oh, I hope she sings the love theme to *The Throat-Punchers*."

Just then, out on the stage, the lights came on and

music began to blare. The show was about to begin. A beautiful cowgirl descended from above on a swing.

It was Dusty Tails herself.

She began to belt out a hard-luck country song. When she came to the chorus, she was joined onstage by a whole gang of dancing Yosemite Sams. D.J. reached out from the wings and yanked one of them backstage. Seconds later, D.J., dressed in a Yosemite Sam costume, was dancing next to Dusty Tails. He managed to dance right up next to her.

"I need to talk to you," he told her urgently. Dusty tried to give him the brush-off, but he hooked her arm in a do-si-do and kept talking. "I'm D.J. Drake," he said. "Damian's son."

Dusty's eyes narrowed. "How do I know —"

Before she could finish her sentence, D.J. whipped off the mask, revealing his face.

"You *are* Damian's son," she gasped.

Backstage after the show, Daffy poked around in Dusty's dressing room while she changed behind a screen and D.J. explained his mission. "I don't have much time. My dad's in trouble. He told me to ask you about the Blue Monkey."

Dusty stuck her head out from behind the screen. "So, then you know?" she asked.

D.J. didn't have a clue what she was talking about. "Oh, yeah," he lied. "Sure. Definitely yes."

"Don't worry about it, D.J." Dusty reassured him. "Your father's the best spy in the agency. They haven't invented a torture yet that could make that man talk."

When he heard the word *spy,* D.J.'s eyebrows shot up in surprise.

"Ha!" Daffy said, jumping around happily. "I was right! And somebody else was wrong! By the process of elimination, that must be —"

"What's the duck talking about?" Dusty asked, poking her head out again.

D.J. grabbed Daffy's bill and twisted it to shut him up. "Nothing," he said. "So, you're a spy, too?"

"Right," Dusty said, from behind the screen. "The pop diva thing, that's only one side of me. I also work for the agency as a professional assassin. It's really hard juggling the two sometimes. I don't know *what* I'll do when I have kids. Oh sure, everybody thinks being a master spy is a piece of cake, but you try dismantling a Uranium grade bomb while your kid's got bubble gum stuck in his hair. And a banana republic is about to go belly-up at the same time my seven year old swallows his allowance — all in small coins! And why does every country have to have civil unrest on a Saturday night? Don't they know how hard it is to book a babysitter?"

D.J. was hardly listening. He was still trying to get used to the idea that his dad really was a spy. "All this time my dad was a spy," he mused, "and I thought he was just a movie star."

Dusty was still talking. "You know how hard it is to find a nanny with advanced weapons training?" she asked. She walked out from behind the screen, dressed in a black leather cat suit. She had on black leather gloves with claws and an infrared scope over one eye. Clearly, she was in spy mode.

Daffy stared at her. His eyes spun like tops. "Woo-hoo! How many galoshes died to make that little number?"

D.J. took in her outfit, too. But he didn't lose focus. "So, what about this Blue Monkey?" he asked.

"Your father's assignment was to track it down before anyone else could find it," Dusty explained. "The diamond has supernatural powers, and it would be a disaster if it fell into the wrong hands. I was supposed to give him this." She reached over to her makeup mirror and pulled out a playing card that had been tucked behind it. Daffy grabbed it before she could hand it to D.J.

"This isn't a king-sized diamond!" he squawked. "This is a queen of diamonds! Whose idea of a sick joke is this?"

Dusty didn't skip a beat. She gave Daffy a karate chop to the head — leaving a visible dent in his feathers — and took the card back.

D.J. reached for it. "I'll take that," he said.

But Dusty shook her head as she stuck the card down her front.

"D.J., you're a nice boy who means well, but face it — if your dad couldn't do it, then it can't be done."

D.J. looked determined. "Maybe. But I'm not gonna let him down."

"Don't worry about it," Dusty assured him. "We've got trained professionals who get paid for this kind of thing."

Daffy had heard enough. He walked over to the door, disgusted. "Some treasure hunt this turned out to be," he complained, as he flung it open.

He found himself staring into the barrel of a cannon.

And Yosemite Sam and his dastardly gang had just lit the fuse.

7. Hit Me

D.J. made a dive for Dusty. He grabbed her and rolled them both out of the way. *POW!* The cannon went off with a bang and a cloud of black smoke. The cannonball flew straight into Daffy, sending him flying into Dusty's makeup mirror and beyond, through the wall and into the showgirls' dressing room. Daffy tipped his hat as he rode the cannonball through the room. "Ladies," he said politely.

Wham! The cannonball kept going, shooting Daffy through another wall and onto the main stage, right through the middle of a big song-and-dance number. Daffy didn't even have time to squawk as he continued to fly through the air, smashing into a glass case that held a big red fire extinguisher. *Phoosh!* Immediately, Daffy and the cannonball were instantly engulfed in a cloud of white foam.

Back in Dusty's dressing room, D.J. let go of the cat-suited singer/spy. But before he got up, he reached over and pulled the playing card from her front. "Thank you," he said with a smile.

Dusty didn't smile back. "You don't know what you're getting into," she warned.

D.J. shrugged. "That's what makes life interesting." He jumped up and headed off, following the Daffy-shaped holes in the walls. Sam and his gang started to follow him, but Dusty Tails went into a one-woman kung fu demonstration that left them lying on the ground, moaning.

D.J. found Daffy covered with foam. When he gave the duck a shake, the white stuff splattered all over. As Daffy spit out a fountain of foam, another cannonball blasted through the wall near them. Sam, Cottontail, and Nasty had recovered, and they weren't far behind!

D.J. and Daffy sprinted up a nearby ladder with Sam and his gang hot on their trail. Up on the second-floor landing, the gang caught up. D.J. gave Cottontail a kick, sending him flying over the railing and down into the casino below. The dirty scoundrel landed in a big cart full of money. Nasty grabbed D.J. Before he could get away, the playing card from Dusty's mirror flew out of his pocket and drifted down, down, down. D.J. grabbed for it and missed. Fighting Nasty off, he leaned over the railing to watch the card fall. Daffy sat on his shoulders to get a better look. Then, without warning, D.J. dove for a chandelier hanging beneath them.

He missed.

Instead of escaping, he landed right in the middle of a poker game at the table under the chandelier. Above him, the elusive card drifted down, landing finally in the stack of cards in front of the dealer. And who was running the show? That regal rooster, Foghorn Leghorn himself.

"Place your bets, gentlemen," said the rooster, as D.J. and Yosemite Sam slipped into the two open seats at the table. Meanwhile, Nasty and Cottontail chased Daffy around the room, throwing sticks of dynamite at the duck and blowing him to pieces over and over again.

Foghorn Leghorn dealt two cards to each player, one up and one down. The game was blackjack. Objective: to take enough "hits" so that your cards add up to twenty-one. The best hand: an ace and a face card.

"Sir?" Foghorn asked D.J., holding out the deck and offering him a card. D.J.'s up card was a two.

"Hit me," D.J. said.

"Don't you want to look at your cards first, son?" Foghorn asked. "Boy's got a lot to learn," he muttered to the other players.

"Just hit me," D.J. repeated. All he wanted was that red-backed queen of diamonds. He knew it was buried in Foghorn's deck.

Foghorn dealt him an ace.

"Hit me again," said D.J.

"Hit *me!*" Sam shouted.

Foghorn Leghorn turned a cold eye on the cartoon cowboy. "Await your turn, sir," he said. He dealt D.J. a card: another ace.

"Hit me," D.J. said, trying to concentrate as Nasty and Cottontail continued to chase Daffy all over the room. "Hit me, hit me, hit me."

"No!" yelled Yosemite Sam, jumping around in a rage. "Hit *me,* frazznabbit!"

"I'll hit you when I hit you," said Foghorn Leghorn. He dealt more cards to D.J.: an ace, another ace, and a two. Sam was furious.

"Hit me," D.J. said, still waiting for his red-backed card. "Hit me, hit me, hit me."

Foghorn dealt: an ace, an ace, and — the queen of diamonds. With a red back.

At that, D.J. turned over his down card. It was an ace.

"Twenty-one!" crowed Foghorn Leghorn. "A winner."

D.J. jumped up and took off with the queen so fast that Foghorn didn't even have time to hand over his winnings. Daffy made up for that by jumping onto the table and sweeping up all the chips, then dashing off with Nasty and Cottontail on his tail.

Sam shrugged and got up to leave. But first, he took one last peek at his bottom card. "Hit me," he said.

With that, Foghorn picked the little cowboy up and spanked him with a big wooden plank.

Whack!

Whack!

Whack!

8. You Drive Me Crazy

"Yee-haw!" D.J. cried, as he sprinted out of the Wooden Nickel casino. He dashed to the Gremlin, jumped into the driver's seat, and was about to start it up when Daffy flew through the window, landing on his lap.

"All right!" Daffy yodeled. "Let's see what this spy car can do!" He reached over to turn the key.

The car fell to pieces.

Daffy's bill dropped open. "That's an interesting feature," he remarked.

Just then, gun shots started to whiz over their heads. There was no time to waste. D.J. abandoned the Gremlin. He grabbed Daffy and took off running.

Behind them, Yosemite Sam and his gang arrived at the main entrance just as a valet was about to fetch a celebrity's car. The celebrity? Jeff Gordon, NASCAR racer. He stood there dressed in his racing suit, holding out a ticket. "It's a modified Chevrolet," he was telling the valet, "with logos all over it and a big twenty-four on the side." The valet ran off and reappeared milliseconds later behind the wheel of the race car. As he opened the door for Jeff Gordon, Sam and the gang elbowed their way past the racer and into his car. Before anyone could react, they had zoomed off down the strip.

D.J. and Daffy ran down Fremont Street, home of a crowded bazaar with booths selling everything from Elvis keychains to Wayne Newton CDs. Daffy couldn't help stopping at a vendor selling T-shirts featuring himself, dressed in hip-hop clothes. "How much is this one?" he asked, holding it up, just as a hail of cartoon bullets started flying toward him. In moments the shirt looked like Swiss cheese, and Daffy was running again, with the NASCAR vehicle close behind.

Meanwhile, three blocks away, Kate and Bugs were just arriving in town. They'd had a fabulous ride in the spy car. Bugs had especially enjoyed the part where Kate accidentally entered her thumbprint into the car's computer and her entire life story came over the video screen, including embarrassing episodes from her high school prom. Now Kate was hunched over the wheel, peering up at all the blinking neon as they cruised down the strip. "There's got to be hundreds of hotels and casinos in Las Vegas. We're never going to find that duck!"

Bugs raised an eyebrow. Then he pointed out the window. At that very moment, an arm-waving, screaming Daffy ran into the street. *Splat!* Daffy hit the windshield like a squashed bug.

"Daffy never misses a cue," Bugs said admiringly.

Kate stomped on the brakes, and the spy car screeched to a halt. D.J. ran up, peeled Daffy off the windshield, and chucked him through the car window. Then he opened the door. "Excuse me," he said, unhooking Kate's seat belt and tossing her into the next seat. He jumped in behind the wheel, stepped on the gas, and peeled out, just seconds before the race car came around the corner.

In the backseat, Bugs and Daffy were thrown together as the spy car screeched through a left turn. Instantly, they began to squabble.

Up front, Kate glared at D.J. "So," he asked casually, ignoring her nasty look, "what brings you to Las Vegas? Did you run out of people to fire in the state of California?"

Kate gritted her teeth, furious. "First you steal my duck, then you steal this car," she hissed.

D.J. corrected her. "You can have the duck." He took another hard left turn, and Kate flew into his lap.

She pushed herself away. "Stop this car!" she cried. "Stop!"

"Calm down," said D.J. "I'm a licensed stunt driver."

"You're a security guard!" Kate argued.

D.J. jerked the wheel even harder, sending the spy car rolling onto its side, up onto its roof, onto its other side, and back onto its wheels as it kept traveling straight ahead. He grinned over at Kate. "Pretty nifty, huh?"

Kate didn't answer. She was in shock.

Bugs poked his head into the front seat. "I'm curious," he said. "Are we gonna stop before we hit that wall? I gotta make arrangements, either way."

Sure enough, the car was headed straight for the back wall of Sam's casino.

Daffy peeked through the windshield. "Mother," he pleaded, covering his eyes.

With that, the dashboard flickered into life. "Taking you to Mother," said a soothing female voice. Flames shot out of the back of the car as the roar of a jet filled the air. The car lifted off — just as the race car came up behind it — and flew up and over the building. It kept climbing, disappearing into the blue sky.

At the wheel of the NASCAR vehicle, Yosemite Sam stared up at the flying spy car. *Crash!* He smashed through the casino wall and raced through the place, scattering showgirls and gamblers every which way.

Up in the sky, the spy car rocketed along smoothly. Kate turned to D.J. "Now *this* is impressive."

D.J. shrugged. "I didn't do anything," he said.

"So, licensed stunt man, what are your plans, if I may ask? Unless your plan is to kill us all, in which case I have to admit this is a magnificent plan," said Kate.

"Don't worry," said D.J. "I've played some video games." At that exact moment, the car went into a nose-dive. "Whoa!" D.J. said, screaming along with everybody else. Then he put on the turn signal and hit the brakes. The car kept diving, straight for the empty desert sands below. D.J. glanced at the fuel gauge.

E.

Empty.

What happens when a spy car runs out of gas? Suddenly, the engine died with a last sputter, and the lights went out. The car screeched to a stop — three feet from the ground.

Bugs grinned as he climbed over Kate and stepped out. "That gag's sixty years old, and it still works!" He gazed around, taking in the view as he leaned on the car's hood.

Wham! The spy car fell the rest of the way to the ground, landing with a crash on the desert sand.

A few hours later, the hot sun blazed down on the foursome as they sat panting in the middle of nowhere, trying to find shade beneath a tall cactus. Two vultures sat hunched above them, staring down hungrily.

"Quit drooling!" Bugs yelled up at them. "I'll *tell* you when I'm dead!"

Meanwhile, Kate was messing with her cell phone, punching button after button. "No service!" she muttered. "What are we, on Mars?" She tossed the phone down and began to cry. "This wasn't the plan!" she wailed. "I'm supposed to start my own production company in two years, meet a rich man, get married, then have two babies, a boy and a girl. I'm *not* supposed to be dying in the desert with a rabbit and a duck and a handsome yet goofy unemployed person!"

Next to her, Daffy sighed wistfully. "I was going to be a dancer," he confessed.

D.J. strolled over, back from a scouting trip. "There's nothing for miles in that, that, or that direction," he said, pointing north, east, and west. "So I suggest we go *that* way." He looked south.

Bugs went all dramatic. "Who you kiddin', doc?" he asked, throwing himself at D.J.'s knees. "We're gonna die out here, alone, our dramatic death throes unseen by the voting members of the Motion Picture Academy!" He passed a hand over his brow. "Water," he cried weakly. "Water!"

D.J. wasn't listening. He was staring at the horizon. "Hey, look!" he said.

There, glistening like a palace in the distance, was a massive megastore. No road, no parking lot, just the store.

Daffy led the stampede. "Water!" he cried. "Sparkling beverages! Juice products!"

Moments later, all four of our heroes reappeared outside the store, dressed in desert-worthy outfits and carrying enough snacks and drinks to keep them alive and happy for a month.

9. Back at Acme

Unless, of course, the forces of evil had their way. Back in the Acme boardroom, Mr. Chairman was interrogating Yosemite Sam. "How did this happen?" he roared, pointing to a hologram of the four escapees standing in front of the store.

"Mistakes were made," Sam admitted. "By others."

Mr. Chairman frowned. So did the big black raven perched on his shoulder. "Thank you for your report," he said, dismissing Sam. He turned to the board. "It now appears that in order to obtain the location of the Blue Monkey, we will have to do away with two people, a rabbit, and a duck. Any problem with that?"

The board members just laughed.

"Unless," said Mr. Chairman, turning to Damian Drake, who was hanging in a cage nearby, "you would like to save us the bother of eliminating your son?" A dungeonmaster stood nearby, arranging an array of torture instruments.

Damian Drake didn't even blink. "My son is going to kick your evil butt!" he shouted.

Mr. Chairman chuckled. Then he frowned. He was clearly just the teensiest bit worried.

One of the board members spoke up. "Uh, Mr. Chairman?" he suggested. "Perhaps we should activate our desert operative."

The rest of the board members rolled their eyes.

"He's due for a win," the man reminded them.

Mr. Chairman reached for the phone.

Out in the hot blazing desert, Wile E. Coyote stopped short and let the Road Runner get away as he reached into a cactus to pick up the receiver. "Hello?" he asked.

When he hung up, the coyote reached for a pair of binoculars. He swept the horizon and focused in on the foursome he'd been ordered to crush. He chuckled to himself as he swapped the binoculars for a laptop. He pecked away fiendishly at the keyboard until a web site came up: Acme. For all your mayhem needs. A quick search brought up the page for Acme's Armored Rocket Launcher and Sports Utility Vehicle. Wile E. Coyote clicked on the Buy icon.

A window popped up. Would you like it gift wrapped? it asked. Another pop-up blinked FREE in red letters. The coyote clicked on the Yes button.

Your order is on its way! read a window on the screen.

Smiling gleefully, Wile E. rubbed his hands together. Seconds later, a wooden crate the size of a small building dropped out of the sky, flattening the coyote and every cactus plant nearby.

The box was bedecked with a big red ribbon.

10. Could This Be Love?

Meanwhile, the fab foursome were still standing in the middle of the desert, staring around cluelessly as they bickered.

"You know, Kate," D.J. was saying, "for an executive in charge of a comedy starring a bunny and a duck, you seem a little . . . what's the word?"

"Humorless," Bugs offered.

Daffy joined in. "Stick-in-the-muddy, Crabby Pattyish, sour persimmonized."

"Un-fun," Bugs added, "despotic, non-jolly —"

Kate glared at both of them. "I'm trying to do my *job*," she said. "Which, by the way, does not involve so-called spies, and monkeys, and diamonds."

D.J. cut her off. "I'm doing this for my father!"

Daffy tried to explain. "He desperately hopes he can finally win his papa's love and respect after years of slacking and poor career choices."

D.J. turned to the duck. "You watch too many movies," he said.

Daffy raised his eyebrows. "The lady doth protest too much, methinks," he sputtered.

"That's nothing," Bugs said, yawning. He pointed at Kate. "This one wants to become the most powerful woman in Hollywood just to show those numbskulls back at Cooper High that they shoulda made *her* Homecoming Queen." He'd heard it all during their car ride.

"I gave the best speech!" Kate exploded. Clearly, the trauma was still fresh for her.

"You know," Daffy said to Bugs, "he's no prize either. Cocky for no reason at all, acts without thinking."

Bugs could top that. "She thinks her nose is too big."

D.J. turned to look at Kate's nose, and she smacked him.

"He likes long walks on the beach," Daffy continued.

D.J. stared at him. "You just made that up!"

Bugs and Daffy ignored him. They were on a roll.

"She has a weakness for unemployed guys," Bugs said.

"He has a weakness for being unemployed," Daffy countered.

"Could it be . . ." Bugs began.

"Love?" Daffy and Bugs crooned together.

Kate looked at D.J.

D.J. looked at Kate.

They both made nasty faces.

"Look, we better get moving," D.J. said. "We'll never get out of this desert if we don't."

They walked for a long time. It was hot. Very hot. Unbelievably hot. Kate started to get cranky.

"Look," D.J. told her, "when we get back to civilization, you can take your duck and rabbit and make your little movie. I don't need or want your help in saving my father."

Kate gave him a skeptical look. "You don't *really* believe that Damian Drake was kidnapped, do you?"

"Sure," Daffy spoke up. "I'll believe anything! That's why I have so many wacky adventures!"

As night fell over the desert, the four built a campfire. Bugs and Daffy were on one side, Kate and D.J. on the other.

"Carrot?" Bugs asked, offering one to Daffy.

"No thanks," Daffy replied grumpily.

"Look, Daffy, everyone really wants you back on the set," Bugs told him.

"Flattered though I might be, *flattened* I will not. By anvil, shotgun, or any other torture device I have become so acquainted with in order for *you* to get the laughs," Daffy vowed.

"We share those laughs," Bugs answered, trying to sound sincere. "We're a team, Daff."

"Oh *sure* we do," Daffy snorted. "It's all 'woo-hoo! Woo-hoo! Yuk, yuk!' — and then BAM! WHAM! BLAM!"

"And your tail is on fire," Bugs put in.

"Exactly my point!" Daffy exclaimed.

"No, really, your tail is on fire," Bugs repeated calmly.

Daffy looked back. Sure enough, he'd gotten too close to the fire and his tail had caught fire. "Yow! Woo-hoo! Woo-hoo!" he shrieked, leaping to his feet. He quickly put the fire out and stood there angrily, his butt smoking.

"Daff, you're accident prone," Bugs said knowingly. "It's funny!"

"Look, I'm not saying I can't take it anymore," Daffy sighed. "But just once, I'd like to be the guy who rides off triumphantly into the sunset — without being singed, sliced, or squashed. Is that too much to ask?" Daffy paused and stared at Bugs. "Oh, why am I asking you?" he muttered. "All you have to do is munch on a carrot and people love you." With that, he rolled over and pretended to go to sleep.

Bugs looked at him for a moment, then grabbed his carrot and started munching.

On the other side of the campfire, Kate and D.J. were sitting with a big tarp over their legs for warmth.

53

D.J. sat staring at the playing card. He held it up to the firelight.

"You really think that card is going to help you save your father?" Kate asked.

"Exactly," D.J. said, staring at it intently. Suddenly, he noticed something he hadn't seen before. "Wow! See that?" D.J. exclaimed. He showed the card to Kate. "That's the 'Mona Lisa.' It's in Paris."

Kate peered at the card. Sure enough, barely visible underneath the Queen of Diamond's face was a miniature of the famous painting.

"Look, I was never great in geography, but isn't France really, really far away from Hollywood?" Kate asked.

"Let me tell you something about myself," D.J. said, impassioned. "There's no distance I wouldn't travel, no mountain I wouldn't climb, no river I wouldn't swim across . . ."

"No hopscotch board . . ." Bugs added.

"No hopscotch board I wouldn't hop across, no . . ."

"Garden gnome," Daffy said.

"No garden gnome I wouldn't step over to help my dad. So if you think I'm not going to Paris, you're sorely mistaken."

Daffy popped up from nowhere and grabbed the card from him. "Whatever! I'm going to get that diamond."

"Not so fast! Get back here with my card!" D.J. yelled.

"Hold it right there, duckface! You're not going anywhere without *MOI*!" Kate shouted at the same time.

"Or *moi*," Bugs said, grinning. He snapped his fingers, and instantly they were in Paris!

11. Paris in the Springtime

D.J., Kate, Bugs, and Daffy found themselves outside a gift shop in the Louvre, the famous museum that housed the "Mona Lisa."

"We're in Paris!" Kate cried.

"I know it defies the law of physics, but I never studied law," Bugs said.

D.J. grabbed a packet about the museum from the Information Desk. "'Mona Lisa,' 'Mona Lisa,' where are you?" he muttered.

A French woman in a black beret walked up to him. "Le skunk dolls are all the rage," she whispered in his ear.

"Uh, thanks for the hot tip," D.J. said, looking confused. "But I'm in the middle of something." Then he went back to his map of the museum.

The French woman rolled her eyes, grabbed D.J.'s arm, and dragged him into a gift store called "Pepé Le

Q's." There were racks and racks of postcards, keychains, and plush toys. The French woman picked a stuffed Pepé Le Pew doll up and handed it to D.J. "Pull zee cord," she told him.

D.J. pulled the cord. "*Bonjour,* Monsieur Drake," the toy said. "I am impressed you made it zis far."

"So I was right!" D.J. exclaimed. "The Blue Monkey is here."

From the other side of the store, Daffy watched D.J. talking to the doll and shook his head sadly. "I leave this guy alone for one second and he starts playing with dolls."

D.J. pulled the cord again. "To find ze Blue Monkey you must . . ." The doll ran out of steam. D.J. pulled the cord again. ". . . view le 'Mona Lisa' through le playing card. It is the window that lies behind her smile. But the most important thing . . ." the doll trailed off.

D.J. tried pulling the cord again, but it snapped in his hand. "Great," he sighed.

Suddenly, the real Pepé Le Pew burst out from behind a counter in the store. "*Sacre bleu!* Le time waster. Go to ze dressing room."

D.J. quickly ducked into the dressing room. It turned out to be a secret arsenal of futuristic weapons and technology! Pepé showed him an array of gadgets he could use for his spy mission.

57

"Yeah, I was thinking I might need a flame thrower, a grenade launcher, some . . ." he trailed off as Pepé handed him a pair of ordinary-looking pants. "Pants?"

"You are not an agent, you do not get le weapon," Pepé told him. "Be careful with zose. Zey are rocket-powered."

D.J. shrugged and tried on the pants. Moments later, Kate, Bugs, Daffy, and D.J. (in the pants) found themselves in a small gallery in front of the world's most famous painting.

The "Mona Lisa."

D.J. looked down at the playing card in his hand, then back at the painting. "Window," he muttered. "Not much of a window." Then he looked closer at the card. There was something about it, a strange sheen that reflected the painting of the mysterious woman and her mysterious smile. D.J. picked at a corner of the card and peeled a clear sheet off the back of it.

"Aha!" Daffy cried. "A window!"

D.J. held up the "window" in front of the painting. Magically, a map appeared. It was an ancient map, but the continent it showed was unmistakable.

Africa.

"Wow!" said D.J.

"Cool!" Daffy added. "Now all we have to do is steal the 'Mona Lisa'!"

The two bored, yawning guards nearby perked up a little. They gazed at the foursome for a moment, then went back to yawning.

Bugs took a look through the window. "We could take a picture through this," he murmured.

Daffy's eyes lit up. "Yeah! Use your spy phone!"

D.J. pulled out the phone and examined its controls. "It doesn't seem to have a camera," he said. He pushed a few buttons. "Maybe this one?" A liquid squirted out, hitting Daffy in the face and melting his bill off. "No," D.J. said. "That one just shoots acid."

Kate pulled out her cell phone and pointed to the camera lens on it. "Spy phone without a camera?" she asked D.J. playfully. "Loser!"

Bugs held up the window, and Kate snapped a picture.

"I-I-I'll take that," someone said.

Kate whirled around to see Elmer Fudd standing there: shotgun, earflaps, and all. The shotgun was aimed straight at Kate.

"What gives, doc?" Bugs asked. "We've made a hundred pictures together. I've loaned you money! I helped hook up your stereo!"

Elmer shrugged. "Well," he said, "as it tuwns out, I'm secwetly evil."

"That's showbiz for you," Daffy said, throwing up his hands.

Elmer re-aimed the shotgun. "Now, make with the card so I can pwease my dark masters."

Bugs went into street-magician mode, adding the red-backed card to a deck and fanning them out. "Pick a card, any card. Then just put it back into the pack. Anywhere is fine."

Elmer looked a little confused. But he stuck the card he held into Bugs's deck. Bugs started to shuffle the cards — behind his back, over his head, *through* Elmer's head. "And, upsie-daisy!" he cried finally, throwing the whole deck up in the air. He reached out to snatch the first card that came fluttering down. "This your card?" he asked Elmer.

"No."

Bugs licked the card and slapped it onto Elmer's forehead. Then he grabbed another and another and another out of the air.

"This your card?"

"No."

"This?"

"No."

"This?"

"No."

Soon Elmer's face was completely covered with cards. Bugs grabbed one last card out of the air. The queen of diamonds.

By then, Elmer couldn't see a thing.

Bugs took Daffy's hand and the two of them ran off, with D.J. and Kate dashing after them.

"It's the queen of diamonds, I tell you!" Elmer cried. He stood there, waiting for a reply. Then he realized he'd been tricked. "Grrr," he said, shaking the cards off his face. "I'm gonna blast that wabbit."

He took off, shotgun in hand, chasing the gang through the museum. Up and down the stairs, through every gallery, past many of the most famous master-pieces in the world.

Kate and D.J. managed to escape around a corner. "Maybe we should go back and help them," D.J. said, looking back the way they'd come. Elmer was right be-hind Daffy and Bugs.

"Nah," Kate said confidently, "Elmer never gets Bugs. It's a formula, but it works."

D.J. glanced back again. At that moment, a hand reached around the corner, covering Kate's mouth with a handkerchief. For a second, she looked surprised.

Then she passed out.

The hand pulled her away, around the corner.

"That's the great thing about movies," D.J. was say-ing. "You always know what's going to happen. For ex-ample" — he paused for a moment — "if this was a movie, you and I would definitely end up together." He glanced over at Kate to see the look on her face. Would she be horrified? Or happy that he'd said it first?

Kate wasn't there.

"Kate?" D.J. ran around the corner just in time to see the unmistakable bulk of Mr. Smith, carrying Kate over his shoulder. He vanished into an elevator.

D.J. dashed for the stairs and got to the main floor just after the elevator arrived. Mr. Smith, still carrying Kate, was just disappearing through the main exit. D.J. took off after them.

Out on the street, Mr. Smith was stuffing a still-unconscious Kate into a burlap sack. He threw her over his shoulder and ran toward the Eiffel Tower.

D.J. raced onto the sidewalk, waving his arms and shouting. "Gendarme!" he cried, spotting Pepé Le Pew riding by on a scooter. The suave skunk was dressed in a French policeman's uniform.

"You have policing needs?" Pepé asked politely.

"That man has a woman tied up in a burlap sack and is taking her to the Eiffel Tower!" shouted D.J., pointing to Mr. Smith.

"Ah!" cried Pepé. "It is spring, is it not?" He scooted away. D.J. looked angry — then ran after Kate and Mr. Smith.

Back inside, Daffy and Bugs were still on the run. Their dash through the museum had turned into a lesson in art appreciation: they'd learned about everything from expressionism to surrealism. At the moment, they were in

When the Warner Brothers fired Daffy Duck, he refused to take it lying down!

Daffy wanted security guard DJ to help him get his job back. But DJ had another mission in mind — saving his father, superspy Damian Drake, from the clutches of the evil ACME Corporation.

Meanwhile, the Warner Brothers sent one of their employees, Kate, to DJ's house to find Daffy. But Bugs kept popping up instead.

DJ and Daffy went to Las Vegas, searching for the clue that would lead them to Damian Drake and the Blue Monkey diamond.

Kate, Bugs, Daffy, and DJ all finally met up in the desert. Then they were off to Paris!

The gang finally located the information they needed in the Louvre, the famous French museum. But unfortunately, the ACME agent Elmer Fudd found them there!

Our heroes. managed to escape Elmer. The next stop on their quest was the African jungle.

At last, DJ, Kate, Bugs, and Daffy found the Blue Monkey diamond!

the middle of learning all about Pointillism. They sat inside a painting of a picnic on the banks of a river. "Pointillism," Bugs lectured to Daffy. "A technique of using individual dots which, taken together, make an image."

Elmer came up behind them in the painting. Bugs whipped out a fan and aimed it at Elmer, who blew away in a swirl of dots.

Meanwhile, D.J. sprinted through the streets of Paris after Kate and Mr. Smith. Finally, he was at the base of the Eiffel Tower. The structure loomed above, a spiderweb of intertwined iron. Overhead, there was the sound of chopper blades as a black helicopter approached.

D.J. had a bad feeling about that helicopter.

He arrived at the entrance to the tower just as Mr. Smith carried Kate into the elevator that zoomed tourists to the observation deck.

D.J. panicked. There was no doubt in his mind that the elevator was headed for a meeting with the helicopter! And he'd never catch up, now. Unless . . . He remembered the special pants Pepé had given him. Now was the moment to try them out!

He looked down at his waistband and pushed the button at the top of his fly. Suddenly, rocket flames shot out of the back pockets of his pants! How cool was that?

D.J. squatted, ready to take off.

Unfortunately, the pants took off without him, roaring into the sky.

That left D.J. in his boxers.

He walked into the elevator, whistling casually as he tried to ignore the crowd of staring tourists.

Up on the observation deck, Mr. Smith held Kate tight as the big black helicopter hovered closer and closer. He slipped the cell phone from her purse and put it into his pocket. Then he reached out for the ladder being lowered from the helicopter.

A hand tapped his shoulder.

He turned.

D.J.'s fist slammed into his face.

Mr. Smith fought back, kicking and punching like a kung fu master even though he still held Kate under one arm. D.J. fell to the ground, overcome by the flurry of punches.

Mr. Smith headed back to the ladder. Kate woke up then, just in time to see where she was: hanging in space, high above the earth, between a spindly tower and a black helicopter. She began to struggle.

Mr. Smith tightened his grip on her and reached for the ladder. Just then, something hit him in the back of the head.

It was a tiny bronze replica of the Eiffel Tower. Annoyed, he turned to see where it had come from — just in time to get hit by another one, this time in silver.

There was D.J. at the gift shop, buying model after model from the salesgirl and hurling each one at his enemy. "Give me the girl!" he shouted. "She's not worth it. She can be extremely annoying!"

Kate, still in Mr. Smith's grip, glared at D.J.

Mr. Smith just shrugged. He turned to grab the helicopter ladder and swung himself up, letting go of Kate as he flew off in the big black bird.

D.J. jumped off the tower to catch Kate. He flew off the ledge in a swan dive.

Screaming, Kate plummeted downward.

D.J. dove after her, pushing a button on his cell phone. The display read RAPPELLING LINE ACTIVATED, as a rope shot out and wrapped around a nearby girder.

The line grabbed.

D.J. swung down to snatch Kate out of thin air.

The line held, and the two of them swung gently to and fro, high above the twinkling lights of Paris.

Then they dipped, swinging low. D.J. plucked a bunch of roses from the hand of a flower girl selling bouquets at the base of the tower. He handed them to Kate, who smiled into his eyes as she sniffed their delicious fragrance. D.J. and Kate swung back and forth, gazing at each other happily.

12. Where to Next?

At a table for four in a little café down the street, Bugs and Daffy were waiting impatiently. They had managed to lose Elmer in the Louvre.

Suddenly, Kate and D.J. landed with a thud in the two empty chairs. Kate put her bouquet on the table. D.J. added a box of chocolates. Then he started talking as if nothing strange had just happened.

"Okay," he said, sounding hopeless, "they've got the cell phone, which means they have the map."

"We've still got that window thingy," said Daffy. "We can take another picture."

D.J. was mad at himself for messing up. "My dad wouldn't have let them get away with the cell phone," he muttered.

"But that's what makes you, you," Bugs said, trying to comfort him.

Kate looked into D.J.'s eyes. "One thing your father would never do is give up," she said firmly.

He shook his head. "You don't know my father," he said.

"But I've seen all his movies!" Kate answered brightly.

D.J. thought for a second. Then he stood up, bracing his shoulders. "You're right!" he said. "Let's go."

Kate and Bugs stood up, too, throwing their shoulders back as they marched off, following D.J.

Daffy jumped up. "We're going to a Damian Drake movie?" he asked hopefully, scampering after the others.

But D.J. had another destination in mind.

Meanwhile, in the penthouse suite of the tallest office building in Paris — the Acme Corporation's French headquarters — the forces of evil were making their own plans.

"Friends," said Mr. Chairman, who sat at the head of the table stroking a furry baby Tasmanian Devil, "I reveal to you the whereabouts of the Blue Monkey."

He pushed a button on the stolen phone/camera, which Mr. Smith had plugged into a console next to him.

A picture appeared before the group. On the right was the beautiful old map of Africa. On the left, Daffy's right eye stared wildly into the camera.

Mr. Chairman looked at the map angrily. Now he

knew that his enemies knew where the Blue Monkey was. "How can I be expected to run a multinational evil corporation with such incompetence?" he roared. "We *cannot* allow some boy and girl and duck and rabbit to thwart our plan for global domination."

"Wanna bet?"

The question came from Damian Drake, who was strapped to a gurney. Next to him was a mad scientist with wild white hair. The man chuckled as he mixed an evil potion.

Mr. Chairman turned to look at Damian. "Five dollars?" he offered.

"You're on," Damian answered.

Mr. Chairman smiled a thin evil smile. "I believe I will hedge my bet. Let us unleash our most vicious operative." He pushed a button, and a large cage descended from the ceiling. Inside was a wild-eyed Taz, snarling and snapping and shaking the bars to get out.

One of the vice presidents spoke up. "Mr. Chairman, I agree that the Tasmanian Devil is quite vicious. But if memory serves, he's also extremely stupid."

Mr. Chairman pushed another button.

The cage opened.

Spinning at the speed of light, Taz flew out toward the vice president.

There was a growling and a gnashing of teeth.

Taz spun back into his cage, licking his lips.

The vice president still sat there — in skeleton form. "I withdraw my objection," he said.

D.J. pushed through the gigantic leaves and looping vines that blocked the path. His safari outfit was soaked with sweat.

Africa.

Kate, Bugs, and Daffy, equally drenched, clustered near D.J. as he hacked his way into a clearing. He pointed his machete toward another thicket of dense jungle. "It's another six thousand cubits in the . . . thick direction," he said.

The others groaned.

Just then, far off in the distance, a distant gnashing could be heard as a fast-moving funnel cloud appeared above the treetops. It came closer and closer, knocking down every bit of vegetation in its path. Herds of animals — wildebeests and gnus, dingoes and lions, boa constrictors and gorillas and chimps — thundered ahead of it, trying desperately to escape.

It came closer, closer.

Finally, the rush of animals passed, and a towering tree toppled over right in front of the foursome. The funnel cloud zipped over it, cutting it neatly in half. Then the tornado came to a stop.

Taz.

Kate just looked at him and shook her head. "You're

another one of those nasty henchmen, aren't you?" she asked.

"Yes ma'am," Taz said politely, slobbering viciously as he pictured his victims roasted and skewered and ready to munch. He began to drool as he imagined Bugs as a delicious roast rabbit, Daffy as a big baked ham, D.J. as a giant hot dog, and Kate as a plump, oozing-with-custard chocolate eclair. Taz shook out a big white napkin, tied it around his neck, and stepped forward, growling.

D.J. pulled the Proboscinator from his pocket and turned it on. He held it up and waved it in Taz's direction. Smell lines radiated out toward the Devil's nose. "Here, boy!" said D.J. enticingly. "You want a treat, boy?"

Taz zoomed up, panting like a pet dog.

"Sit, boy," D.J. commanded. "Beg. Roll over. Back flip."

Taz obeyed. Then he sat up, waiting eagerly for his treat.

D.J. dropped the nose-shaped device right into Taz's wide-open mouth. Taz gobbled it down without even chewing. He licked his lips and turned back, waiting for more.

Then his face changed. A bewildered look came into his eyes. Smell lines began to radiate out from his body. He looked down, just in time to see himself transformed into a golden-brown fragrant roast chicken. "Chicken!" Taz growled happily. And before he could stop himself, he gobbled himself right up, leaving only his mouth behind.

The mouth hung there in the air for a moment, frowning a little.

Then it dropped to the ground and ran off into the jungle, yipping like a dog that's lost its bone.

D.J. dusted off his hands. "Okay, then!" he said happily, picking up his machete. "Let's get back to hacking!"

Hours later, the foursome was still hacking. The vegetation was thicker than ever, and they were getting nowhere. Exhausted, dripping with sweat, and getting crankier by the minute, they swung their machetes automatically, hardly noticing where they were cutting.

Daffy took a big swing and lopped off Bugs's tail.

"Hey!" Bugs cried indignantly.

"Sorry, old chap," Daffy apologized, as Bugs slapped his tail back on.

Behind them, Kate slumped to the ground. "I can't go on any further," she wailed.

Daffy plopped down next to her. "And I'm not leaving her here," he declared.

CRASH! Something was stomping toward them,

thrashing its way through the jungle. Something big. Something gargantuan.

With a loud trumpeting call, an elephant burst through the underbrush, its trunk held high. It loomed above them, as big as a truck.

And it was headed straight for Kate.

13. Monkeying Around

"Bad elephant!" somebody yelled.

It wasn't Bugs.

Or Daffy.

Or D.J.

Or Kate.

It was Tweety! The little yellow bird swung inside his cage, which was perched on top of the elephant's massive head. "You almost stepped on those people!" he added chirpily.

As the elephant came closer, D.J. and the others could see Granny sitting on his back, with Sylvester curled up next to her. Granny was all decked out in the latest safari gear. "Little Damian!" she cried. "How funny seeing you here! You look exhausted, dear. Would you like a lift?"

Daffy didn't waste any time. He jumped up to sit behind Granny before she even finished her sentence.

"Giddyap," he shouted, kicking his heels into the elephant's sides. The elephant did not seem to notice.

Bugs jumped aboard, too. "It sure was a lucky coincidence, you showing up just now," he said to Granny.

She just smiled, a mysterious little smile. "Yes," she said calmly. "Wasn't it?"

The others climbed on, and Granny steered the elephant through the jungle. Sightseeing from the back of an elephant turned out to be a whole lot more fun than hacking through the jungle. The best part was when they passed a spreading tree full of dozens of birds that looked just like Tweety, only in every color of the rainbow. "I've discovered my roots!" Tweety said, looking up at them wide-eyed.

"And I've discovered my dinner," said Sylvester, licking his lips. He crouched down, getting ready to pounce.

All the Tweetys twittered at once, then flew down and pecked Sylvester until all he had left was a few tufts of fur. Tweety laughed and laughed.

The elephant lumbered along until, finally, it pushed through one last thick patch of jungle and entered a clearing.

Kate gasped. They stood facing a vast plaza. It was an ancient city of stone, surrounded by giant stone monkeys. Their wise old faces gazed down on the ruins they guarded.

"Looks like this is our stop," said D.J. He pulled out his wallet.

"Oh, put your money away," Tweety insisted.

Granny agreed. "It was our pleasure," she said. "Enjoy the rest of your adventure."

The foursome climbed down from the elephant and waved good-bye as it lumbered back into the dense underbrush surrounding the ancient city. Then D.J. put his arm around Kate, and they both gazed into the long tall corridor that lay in front of them. At its end was a stone monkey altar.

It was bathed in a brilliant blue glow.

"It's mine!" Daffy shouted, dashing past them. "All mine!"

D.J. grabbed him by the tail feathers. Holding the excited duck upside down, he pointed out a sign at the opening of the corridor.

It read GAUNTLET OF DEATH. YOU MUST BE AT LEAST THIS TALL TO DIE HORRIBLY.

Daffy took a closer look at the walls of the corridor, which were covered with drawings of horrifying monsters and scary skeletons. He blinked when he saw an image of a duck skull. "You know," he said, still hanging upside down, "I hadn't noticed that."

Just then, a volcano in the distance gave off a loud rumbling, and flaming lava began to flow down its sides.

D.J. let go of Daffy, dropping him on his head. He picked up a coconut lying nearby and threw it into the gauntlet. It was impaled in midair by a trap that sprang out of nowhere. Coconut milk started spurting out of it.

Bugs grimaced. "Well," he said. "That explains all the skeletons."

D.J. began to walk into the gauntlet.

"D.J.!" cried Kate. "What are you, a maniac?"

He turned for a second. "I'm a *trained* maniac," he informed her solemnly. He kept moving very slowly and carefully, dodging each trap as he activated it. Spikes came down out of the ceiling, darts flew out of the walls. D.J. avoided them all.

Daffy got impatient. "For crying out loud!" he yelled. "Time is moolah! Get the lead out!" He clapped his hands together, urging D.J. on like a baseball coach on the sidelines.

D.J. ignored him. He was busy tiptoeing, very precisely, through a writhing tangle of poisonous snakes.

"C'mon," Daffy yelled again. "Move it! My greed needs to be slaked!"

D.J. stopped for a second to look back at him. "Relax," he told the duck. "This is going to take a few hours."

Daffy went nuts. "A few *hours*? Forget that, mister!" He stormed ahead, marching full tilt into the gauntlet. Every trap came to life at once, bombarding him with darts, swords, explosions, crawling scorpions, shooting flames, sharp knives, tremendous tumbling boulders, and man-eating plants.

Daffy staggered through it all, taking the hits that D.J. was so carefully avoiding. By the end of the line, he was fried to a cinder and as holey as Swiss cheese.

Bugs and Kate walked through the gauntlet after D.J. and Daffy, right past the already-tripped traps. "Bravo!" cried Bugs, applauding D.J.'s heroism.

"It's what I do," D.J. said modestly.

Kate bent over to smile at the nearly destroyed Daffy. "And *you* were pretty funny," she said.

He got to his feet woozily. "It's what I do," he echoed.

Bugs came up behind him. "Nobody takes a deadly blow more hilariously than Daffy," he said, thumping his friend on the shoulder.

Daffy's arm fell off.

D.J. was moving on by then, approaching the blue glow that surrounded a tall pedestal.

Daffy zipped in front of him at lightning speed. Arriving first at the pedestal, he cackled happily. "Hello, wealth and — power?" He stared down at the object on the pedestal. It was nothing but a small blue monkey-shaped stone mounted on a stone ring. Daffy picked it up for a closer look. "This is the Blue Monkey?" he asked, disgusted. "This dime-store bauble? I've been rooked! Cheated by the gods!" He raised his arms heavenward. "Where's my humongous gem?"

Kate stepped forward and plucked the ring out of his hand. "Wait a second," she said. "This is a *tessella!*"

Bugs, D.J., and Daffy just stared at her.

She explained. "A mosaic piece. One of many identical interlocking pieces that form a pattern. First used in Mesopotamia."

The others were still staring.

"See?" she stated. "I don't have an IQ of one hundred six for nothing!" Then she pointed to the mosaic on the wall next to her. "Plus, I noticed there was a piece missing from this one."

The mosaic was made up of interlocking monkey figures, forming one massive monkey shape. Sure enough, one piece in the center was missing. Kate put on the ring. Then she reached out and inserted the monkey on the ring into the empty space.

There was a long, drawn-out creaking sound, as if something ancient were coming to life. Then the entire money-shaped mosaic pushed out of the wall! Kate stepped back, surprised. Her hand was still attached. Thinking quickly, she gave her hand a twist, and the whole mosaic turned as if the ring were a key.

The ground trembled beneath them.

Behind the pedestal, a wall lowered, turning into a bridge across a moat of red-hot, bubbling, molten lava.

Across the moat was the *real* monkey altar, in all its breathtaking glory. In the center of everything was a statue of a giant Buddha monkey. In its hands was a massive sparkling diamond.

"I'm rich! I'm rich!" cried Daffy, dashing over the bridge. He ran up to the altar and headed straight for the Buddha monkey. He dove for the diamond. Suddenly, he stopped in midair.

D.J. had grabbed him.

"If you don't mind," D.J. said formally.

"Mind?" Daffy asked, after D.J. had dropped him to the ground. "I was just poisoned, burnt, chopped, and eaten for that diamond. Why should I mind?"

D.J. didn't answer. He stood in front of the diamond, gazing at it in awe. Carefully, he removed it from the statue's hands and turned it this way and that so that its facets caught the light, glittering like ice in the sun. Then, D.J. saw the image of a monkey's face emerging from the center of the diamond. A blue monkey. D.J. held the diamond high. "This is for you, Dad," he said solemnly.

"That is so sweet," said a voice from behind them. Everyone turned to see who had spoken.

It was Granny, with Sylvester by her side. Tweety sat nearby, in his cage.

"Now," she said, "if you could hand over the diamond . . ."

14. Without a Trace

Granny reached under her chin.

She peeled off her face.

Another face appeared beneath it.

The face of Mr. Chairman.

"Immediately," he said, holding out his hand for the gem.

Next to him, Sylvester opened his mouth wide, and the face of Mr. Smith appeared. The mountainous man wriggled out of his cat costume until he stood as tall and as broad as ever.

Tweety looked shocked. "Hey!" he chirped. "You're not Granny and puddy-tat! What have you done with them, you monsters?"

Mr. Chairman gave an evil laugh. Then he smiled. "Let's just say I sent them on a little vacation."

Tweety smiled back. "Oh. That was very nice of you."

Mr. Chairman turned back to D.J. "The diamond, Mr. Drake." He held out a hand.

"No!" D.J. said. "Forget you! You're evil."

"I see," said Mr. Chairman. "Well, then." He gestured behind him, and Mr. Smith lumbered forward. "Activate the Relocator!" Mr. Chairman ordered.

Mr. Smith touched a red button on a device he wore on his wrist. *ZAP!*

Almost instantaneously, everyone in the area disappeared.

Mr. Chairman was gone.

Mr. Smith was history.

Bugs bugged out.

Daffy dematerialized.

Kate skedaddled.

D.J. disappeared.

15. Choo-Choo!

Just as instantaneously, all six of them reappeared — standing close together inside a machine labeled "Acme Integrator," at Acme headquarters.

But something wasn't quite right.

"Eh — what's up?" Bugs said, staring at the big floppy rabbit ears poking up from Mr. Chairman's head. He felt for his own ears and found a pair of human ears in their place.

D.J. looked cross-eyed at the duck's bill that had landed on his face.

Daffy had two long human arms hanging from his shoulders.

Mr. Chairman frowned, a rabbity buck tooth poking out from between his lips. "I thought we fixed the glitch!" he shouted. He shrugged. "My apologies. At Acme, our focus is really on vision. We're working on the quality controls." He slammed a fist into the Integrator's control panel. Lights blinked on and off as he punched button after button.

Their bodies finally returned to normal. Materialization was complete.

Mr. Chairman took a deep breath. "But enough with the small talk," he continued. "Give me the diamond."

"What diamond?" D.J. asked, all innocent.

"Don't play stupid with me," Mr. Chairman growled.

Bugs leaned against the Integrator, munching a carrot. "Eh, why not, doc?" he asked.

"Because in the game of stupid," Mr. Chairman explained patiently, "there can be only one victor."

Bugs blinked. "Sounds to me like you're afraid of being out-stupided," he observed.

Mr. Chairman exploded. "Nobody out-stupids *me*, Mr. Bunny!" he shouted. "I am the stupidest of them all!"

Bugs raised one eyebrow.

There were snickers from around the room.

That was it for Mr. Chairman. He took a threatening step toward D.J., reaching out to grab the diamond.

D.J. held the sparkling gem high in the air. "Don't come any closer," he said. "Or I'll break it!"

Mr. Chairman stepped back. "I see you require encouragement," he said smoothly. He picked up a remote control and aimed it at a giant TV monitor mounted on the wall.

The monitor came to life. It showed nothing but a small pinprick of light in the center of the screen.

D.J. snorted. "What's that, a firefly?" he asked.

83

"Nah," said Bugs. "Looks more like a night light."

Kate couldn't resist chiming in. "I think it's a distant star," she mused, cocking her head to look at it.

Mr. Chairman pushed a button on the remote and zoomed in, and suddenly everyone in the room could see that the tiny light was actually a headlight on a cute little model train. "It's the Acme Loco-locomotive," explained Mr. Chairman, "from last year's Christmas collection. It wasn't a big seller. Probably something to do with this . . ." He pushed another button.

The charming choo-choo transformed into a hideous death-train, mounted with a rusty, six-bladed buzz saw. The train screeched crazily along the tracks, sparks flying from its wheels.

Mr. Chairman smiled. "And it is heading toward this man," he went on, as the screen changed to show a cavernous warehouse stacked high with boxes and crates.

Inside the warehouse was a train track.

And tied securely to that track was a man.

Damian Drake.

"Do the right thing, Damian Junior!" cried the doomed man, as D.J. stared in horror at his father.

Mr. Chairman chuckled. "Now, I'm no family therapist," he admitted, "but I'd say if you wanted to keep your family 'together,' so to speak . . ." He held out a hand. "I'd give me the diamond, son."

16. The Diabolical Plan Revealed

D.J. thought hard — but only for a moment. Then, slowly and reluctantly, he held out the precious Blue Monkey diamond to Mr. Chairman.

The second Mr. Chairman's hand closed around the diamond, a gang of henchmen rushed forward to grab D.J., Kate, Bugs, and Daffy.

"Hey!" D.J. said, struggling in the henchman's grasp. "What about my dad?"

Mr. Chairman just smiled a slow, calm, extremely evil smile. "He's waiting for a train," he said. Then he turned to another henchman. "Send in Marv."

Moments later, Marvin The Martian burst into the room. "Yes, boss?" he asked.

Mr. Chairman handed him the sparkling gem.

"Ooh," Marvin sighed, stroking it. "Isn't it lovely?"

Mr. Chairman was irritated. "Stop groping it with your sticky little alien hands," he said. "It's unsightly.

Now, run off and install it on the satellite, so I can proceed with my diabolical plan."

At that, Marvin pocketed the gem and marched over to a door marked "Airlock Elevator." With a sudden *whoosh*, he disappeared upwards.

Daffy spluttered and twisted himself out of his guard's grip. "Not while there's Duck Dodgers in the Twenty-fourth and a half Century!" he vowed, snaking his way through the crowd of henchmen. He disappeared into the airlock right behind Marvin and whooshed off. Seconds later, Bugs followed him.

Mr. Chairman stepped to the window and watched as Marvin's spaceship blasted off from the roof of the Acme building. Behind it, Daffy's ship traced a contrail in the sky. Mr. Chairman shrugged. "Your friends' efforts will prove quite futile," he said. He walked over to a table and picked up a model of a satellite in one hand and a model of Marvin's spaceship, the Blue Monkey mounted on the very tip of its nose, in the other.

"You see," he said, "Marvin is about to go up like this," he raised the hand with the spaceship up toward the one with the satellite, "go round and round like that, take this up to that, put it in this, and —"

With a crash, he banged the two models together, a little too hard. Plastic pieces flew around the room.

"At which point," he continued, trying to round up the pieces, "I will broadcast a broad spectrum beam around the world that will change all of the human population into monkeys."

Kate gasped. Mr. Chairman was talking about using a satellite to beam the Blue Monkey's power all over the world! How could the world survive if the entire population went ape? "Okay, so, that's crazy," she said.

"Oh, be honest," said Mr. Chairman. "When you were a kid, didn't you always dream of turning the entire world into monkeys?"

"No," Kate and D.J. said simultaneously.

"Oh. Well, maybe it was just me," replied Mr. Chairman. "Anyway, in the world of the monkey, the human is king. I will be safely protected by my own personal shield."

Mr. Chairman clapped his hands. "Take these future monkeys away!" he ordered.

The henchmen dragged their prisoners off.

17. Duck Dodgers...and a friend

Daffy talked to himself as his ship blasted out of the top of the Acme building, following Marvin's rocket. It felt good to be on his own, about to save the world.

"The lone, intrepid astroduck chases the evil villain," he muttered, already a legend in his own mind.

Just then, Bugs popped up behind Daffy. He squeezed a carrot out of a space-food pack and began to munch. "I was wondering when this flight was gonna take off," he said casually.

"Hey!" spluttered Daffy. "Find your own spaceship, buster!"

Bugs leaned back and crossed his arms. "Nope," he said. "I'm going with you."

"Over my dead carcass!" swore Daffy.

Just then, Marvin swooped by their ship, firing a high-tech laser gun. The blast found its target. Result? Charred Duck.

A blackened Daffy raised one finger. "Motion to strike that last statement from the record!" he pleaded.

Then he looked out the window just in time to see Marvin's spaceship swooping off toward a distant Acme satellite. The Blue Monkey glowed and sparkled from the nose of Marvin's ship.

Daffy looked at Bugs.

Bugs looked at Daffy.

It was time to put their differences aside.

Time to team up.

Time to catch the wily Martian and save the world.

They went into mach speed and roared toward Marvin's ship. Catching up to him right before he reached the satellite, they veered into his ship, creating a shower of sparks as the two ships jostled each other in space. *Slam! Wham!* The two rockets raced along next to each other, jockeying for position as they hurtled toward the satellite.

Marvin thrust his ship into Daffy's, sending it into a tailspin. Then he took off, laughing.

Daffy wrestled with the steering wheel and got his ship under control. In milliseconds, he was right on Marvin's tail again, flashing his high beams into the Martian's mirror.

"Why must they be so irritating?" Marvin groused to himself as Bugs and Daffy pulled up alongside him.

Bugs motioned to him from the other rocketship.

Marvin shrugged.

Bugs motioned again.

Marvin still didn't understand what Bugs was trying to tell him.

Bugs motioned to him to roll down his window.

Marvin sighed. But he cranked the window open. "What is it, annoying earthlings?"

Whooosh! Marvin was sucked out the window of his ship and into deep space.

Daffy stared at Bugs.

"Whaddaya know?" he asked. "He fell for it. Guess I owe you five bucks."

Bugs and Daffy grinned at each other in triumph.

Little did they know that the feisty Martian was clinging like a space barnacle to the bottom of their ship.

18. Some Assembly Required

Back on earth, Kate and D.J. hung suspended from a chain in the Acme warehouse, surrounded by towering stacks of crated Acme goods. D.J. glanced down to see his father lying tied to the train tracks below.

The demonic train, whistle blowing and saw blades spinning, was approaching quickly.

"Don't worry, Dad!" cried D.J. "I'm going to get you out of there!"

"You can get out of this, D.J., I know it," Damian called to his son. "Just put your mind to it."

D.J. looked at Kate. "If we get out of this, I'd really like to take you to dinner."

Kate smiled. "Invitation accepted."

That settled, D.J. began looking around wildly. How could he save his father?

"Any ideas?" Kate asked.

D.J. didn't have a clue. Then his eye fell on something. He motioned with his head. "See that box over there?" he asked.

Kate looked. There, at the top of one of the stacks, was a box labeled "Acme Laser Cutter." Big red letters surrounded by balloons, spelled out, "No assembly necessary! Assembles itself! Just say, 'Assemble.'"

Kate blinked. "You mean, the one that says 'Acme Voice-Controlled Self-Assembling Laser?'" she asked.

D.J. faced the box. "Assemble!" he commanded.

Nothing happened.

D.J.'s face fell.

Kate sighed. "Look, there's fine print," she pointed out. "Batteries not included."

D.J. rolled his eyes. "Of course."

Just then, they heard something behind them. A rustling sound. And then, the *zing, zing!* of a pneumatic riveter.

"Did you hear that?" Kate asked, as they both turned to see what it was.

Another crate, a huge one, sat high on the pile. This one was labeled, "Acme Robot Guard Dog." The sides of the crate fell open, and a cute but enormous metal guard dog stood before them.

"I always wanted a dog," D.J. said. "Be a good dog and help us down," he called to the dog.

"I'm the Punisher!" he howled. Robotlike, the dog lurched over to where D.J. and Kate hung from the chain. He opened his mouth wide and yanked the chain from the huge iron rafter that it hung from, bending the iron as if it were taffy. He bit through the chain, gulping down the links in one mighty swallow. Then he spit out the links, machine-gun style. They formed words on the warehouse floor: "Bad dog."

The dog dropped D.J. and Kate to the floor and started toward D.J.

"Get! Get out of here now!" D.J. yelled.

The dog shook his head no.

"That's it! You're going straight to obedience school, mister!" shouted Kate.

The dog wanted to play. He whined and pawed the ground. Meanwhile, the train was getting closer and closer.

"I'll distract him!" D.J. yelled. "You go untie my dad!"

D.J. went for the dog and grabbed his tail. "Here you go, boy! Want to play? Let's play chase our own tail, you big metal mutt!"

The dog started chasing his tail in a circle, snapping on it playfully. D.J. held on as tight as he could. It was quite a ride! "Go!" he yelled to Kate.

Kate made a run for it, but the dog was too fast for her. He threw D.J. into a pile of crates and stepped toward her.

"Uh-oh," Kate said nervously. "I think he wants to play with me now!"

19. The End Is Near

High above the warehouse, Marvin's empty ship continued its race toward the massive Acme satellite. "Auto Pilot," said a blinking light on the dashboard. The Blue Monkey was still on course. Mr. Chairman's diabolical plan was still in motion.

Bugs and Daffy chased after it, but they arrived seconds too late. Marvin's ship was docking with the satellite when they arrived. They watched in awe as the huge satellite transformed, sprouting radar dishes and two enormous solar panels that doubled as electronic billboards. "Eat at Joe's," read one. "Your Ad Here," said the other.

Marvin's ship, carrying the Blue Monkey, was already activating the satellite. The process had to be stopped.

But who would save the world — and how?

Bugs reached into the back seat for an individual jet pack.

Daffy grabbed it from him.

"In case you haven't guessed by now," Daffy said indignantly, "I'm tired of being your second banana. If you think I'm going to let you strap on this rocket pack, jet into space, and risk your life scaling that . . . that . . ."

He gulped as he looked up at the looming satellite. It seemed as big as the moon, up close. With a quick change of heart, he set the jet pack onto Bugs's back. "You're darn right," he finished. "Bugs," he went on, as he pulled the straps tight, "you may not know this, but beneath this macho exterior, I'm actually a scared-to-death, brazen little coward. So, good luck, buddy!" He gave the jet pack a slap and turned it on.

Bugs climbed out onto the round roof of their spaceship — and found himself looking down the barrel of a ray gun.

He turned to face Marvin. "Eh, what's up, doc?" he asked.

Marvin was angry. "You tricked me," he said. "And that wasn't nice. Now I must incapacitate you with my bubble gun." He began to pump his ray gun. Pink bubbles formed in its clear chamber.

Bugs frowned. "Pity I got a rotten bicuspid," he drawled. "You got that in sugarless?"

Marvin looked at him. "Hmmm," he said, handing the gun to Bugs. "Hold this a minute, will you?"

Bugs smiled. "What a space case," he muttered to himself, as Marvin rummaged around in his pack.

The Martian took out another gun, this one labeled, "Sugarless Bubble Gun." Pumping it, he shot off a chain of Bugs-sized Bubbles.

Bugs dodged and pumped his own gun, aiming back at Marvin.

Bubbles filled the air as they both fired away.

Bugs's foot got caught in a bubble.

He dodged another, swinging his foot up so that it touched Marvin's head. The bubble on his foot caught Marvin. Slowly, the rabbit and the Martian drifted away into the deep blackness of space, joined by their bubbles.

But Marvin had not forgotten his mission. He reached down to a button on his belt and pushed it.

Above them, a mechanical arm grabbed the Blue Monkey from the nose of Marvin's spaceship and began to install it on the satellite.

Meanwhile, Daffy lay curled up inside his own spaceship, sucking his thumb. He glanced up just in time to see Bugs float by, surrounded by a pink bubble. Bugs was trapped! Mr. Chairman's plan was going to succeed — unless someone else took action. Daffy blinked once, twice. Then he sat up and began to talk to himself.

"You wanna be second banana all your life?" he asked.

"Yep, you bet," he answered himself.

"No, you don't!" Daffy shouted to himself.

"Sure I do," he retorted.

"No, no!" Daffy insisted to himself.

Daffy stood up. "Yes!" he declared, in a ringing voice. He'd won the argument with himself. "I'm going to be the hero of this adventure!"

He reached for a jet pack and strapped it on.

"Duck Dodgers, to the rescue!" he cried.

Blam!

The jet pack exploded.

Daffy stood reeling, his feathers crispy. He grabbed another jet pack. "Duck Dodgers to the rescue!" he said, a little less bravely.

Kaboom!

Daffy staggered around for a moment, gathering his wits. He picked up another jet pack. "Duck Dodgers to the rescue?" he bleated.

Bang!

Daffy spun around three times and ended up sitting in a heap. He put on one more jet pack. This time he put his fingers in his ears. "Whatever," he said wearily.

BABOOM!!!

20. In the Nick of Time

Down in the warehouse, the train was getting closer and closer to Damian Drake. And Kate was still cornered by the dog. "I'm really more of a giant robot cat person," she told the dog anxiously.

The dog licked her cheerfully — and lifted her off the ground! Kate turned and fled up a pile of crates.

Meanwhile, D.J. was stumbling woozily to his feet. He saw a hook dangling from a cable and grabbed it! He swung across the warehouse like Tarzan and swooped down on the dog. In a blur, he attached the hook to the dog's collar. Then he made a dash for his dad. The train was bearing down on him!

The dog didn't care. He was up and after D.J. in a flash. The chain D.J. had linked to his dog collar held him back! The dog was stopped in his tracks, growling and gnashing his mechanical teeth.

Meanwhile, D.J. was moving like a trained stuntman. Nothing could stop him from saving his dad —

nothing! He plunged toward his dad as the train grew ever closer. Kate screamed as she watched him dive toward certain death. As the train hurtled toward his dad, D.J. whipped out his cell phone and, moving at light speed, used its built-in picklock to undo his dad's chains. They were both saved!

Damian Drake looked at his son in surprise and admiration. "That's as close a call as I've ever had. Well done, son."

D.J. just shrugged. "If we wait around here any longer, we'll all be monkeys. Let's go!"

21. Saved by the Bill

Bugs and Marvin drifted along in their bubbles, still shooting at each other as they floated past the satellite.

Beneath them, Daffy blasted out of the ship, heading straight for the robot arm holding the Blue Monkey. The arm was busy installing the diamond into the Beam Projector, the laser that would shoot out the gem's horrible power all over the world.

Marvin spotted Daffy out of the corner of his eye. Reaching down, he pushed another button on his belt.

Daffy was closing in on the Blue Monkey. He could almost reach out and touch it. "Proving once and for all," he narrated to himself, "that right triumphs over —"

Just then, the giant solar panels swung shut, slapping together like a giant flyswatter. In a moment they opened again, resuming their positions.

Like a dead fly, Daffy spiraled down, down, down, onto a deck of the satellite. He reached out to grab onto something, anything. ". . . might," he finished, a dazed look on his crumpled face.

Meanwhile, Marvin was still firing away at Bugs. Pink bubbles floated everywhere, but that didn't keep the Martian from seeing that it was time for the next step in Mr. Chairman's diabolical plan. He started toward the satellite, pressing one more button on his belt.

Above Daffy, two gigantic Tesla coils began to hum with electricity. The laser was starting to power up, and anything that got in the power's way would be fried. Daffy glanced up at the coils. Then he pulled his cape over his head. "Static-cling free," he boasted.

Seconds later, huge bolts of electricity engulfed him completely, zapping him with thousands of volts. When the smoked cleared, Daffy's cape still stood tall.

But beneath it, there was nothing but a heap of ash.

Above the heap, a duck's bill floated lazily in space.

Daffy reached up a hand from the ashes and grabbed the duck bill. Burnt, weak, nearly done in, Daffy looked up at the gigantic Beam Projector, where the Blue Monkey was now securely in place.

He looked down at the bill in his hand.

With his last ounce of strength, he reached back and hurled the bill high into space. It looked like a boomerang as it sped through the unending blackness toward the Beam Projector.

The bill twirled as it flew.

Daffy watched, a faint gleam of hope lighting his eyes.

Then the bill landed — right in the middle of the Beam Projector's lens. At that very moment, the power came on and the Projector lit up.

But there was no huge, powerful, world-engulfing beam.

Instead, there were only two, tiny pencil-thin beams of blue light firing out of the nostrils of Daffy's beak.

One went off into space.

The other hit somewhere on earth.

"You did it!" a bill-less Daffy cried to himself.

"I did?"

"You did!"

22. No More Monkeying Around

At that very moment, down at Acme headquarters, the door of Mr. Chairman's Shield Chamber flew open and Mr. Chairman stepped out, rubbing his hands gleefully.

"Open for business!" he said happily.

Then he spotted D.J., Kate, and Damian standing in his boardroom. His face fell when he realized they had not transformed.

"Why aren't you monkeys?" he asked wildly.

He backed away from them, a frightened look on his face. Just then, a thin shaft of blue light shone through the window behind him.

Instantly, Mr. Chairman morphed into a monkey.

"Arrggghhh!" he cried, looking down at his hairy hands and arms.

23. A Duck and His Bill, Reunited

Overhead, the situation was critical. Daffy's bill was still attached to the Projector Beam, but it was under tremendous pressure. It glowed bright blue as the massive energy dammed up behind it tried to escape.

OVERLOAD, flashed a red sign on the satellite's control panel.

Bolts of electricity arced back and forth along the satellite.

Marvin worked furiously at the controls, punching buttons and twirling dials in a last-ditch effort to stabilize the satellite.

Then, with a noise like a champagne cork popping, the bill popped off the Projector and landed back on Daffy's face.

Smiling, Daffy pulled out a tail feather and threw it at Bugs, who was still trapped in a big pink bubble.

The bubble popped, and Bugs fell into Daffy's arms.

"You saved the day, Daffy," Bugs sighed happily.

"Go on, you can say it: 'I'm your hhh . . .'— you know, rhymes with 'zero . . .'" Daffy said smugly.

"Don't push your luck," Bugs told him.

They climbed into their ship and blasted off for earth as, behind them, the satellite continued to go haywire.

Marvin pushed a series of buttons. "Hmmm," he muttered, "there it is. I've discovered the problem." He reached for one last button, but just before he could press it, the satellite exploded into a million fiery bits.

Bugs and Daffy flew off, dodging the debris, as Marvin tumbled down, down, down, afloat on a control panel raft, in a sea of satellite parts.

24. Happily Ever After?

Down in Mr. Chairman's boardroom, Damian put his arm around his son's shoulders. "Now that you've seen what you're capable of," he asked D.J., "what do you want to do with yourself?"

D.J. looked over his father's shoulder, out the window. A spaceship, piloted by Daffy and Bugs, was hurtling toward them at warp speed.

"We should probably move," he said.

Damian was confused. "What's wrong with Beverly Hills?" he asked.

D.J.'s eyes were growing wider as the spaceship approached. "I meant, move from this spot!" he yelled, grabbing his dad and pulling him away from the window just in time.

The spaceship crashed into the boardroom.

Bugs and Daffy opened the hatch and stepped out.

"You're my hero! Go on, say it!" Daffy was saying to Bugs.

"Are you sure?" Bugs asked.

"Positive," Daffy declared.

"I'm your hero," Bugs said, grinning.

"Pronoun trouble," Daffy muttered.

Kate looked at them both proudly. "You guys — I can't believe you did it!"

Daffy blushed. "Yeah, well . . ."

"Good work Daffy," D.J. said. He shook Daffy's hand. "You really came through."

"You're not so bad yourself, stuntboy," Daffy replied. He turned to Bugs. "Shall we?"

"Back to Hollywood," Bugs agreed. He and Daffy waved to the others and walked off together, looking happy.

Damian Drake smiled at Kate, who was gazing at him. She looked a little starstruck. "Well, aren't you going to introduce us, D.J.?"

"Dad, this is Kate; Kate, this is my dad, Damian Drake." D.J. looked a little embarrassed. He was used to being overshadowed by his famous father.

Kate and Damian shook hands. "I'm a really big fan . . . of your son." She looked over at D.J., who looked surprised.

"Me too," said Damian. But Kate and D.J. didn't hear him. D.J. had swept Kate into his arms for a big kiss.

Just then, Damian turned to spot Mr. Chairman, still

in monkey form, trying to sneak away. Damian slapped a pair of handcuffs on him and marched him out of the room.

Meanwhile, Bugs and Daffy were strolling down a long hallway inside the warehouse, trying to find a way out.

"Well, Daff, you didn't get the diamond, but you achieved your goal of becoming a hero," Bugs commented, gnawing on a carrot.

"You know what the best part is?" Daffy answered triumphantly. "You *didn't* achieve *your* goal of getting me back in your movie!"

"And, *cut!*" cried the director. "That's a wrap."

25. The End. Really.

An army of stagehands began working busily to take the set apart.

Filming was over.

Daffy and Bugs shrugged at each other. Then Daffy walked Bugs to his limo. The usual crowd of personal assistants flew around Bugs, opening the door for him, handing him a carrot, wrapping him in a robe.

"You know," Bugs said to Daffy, as he climbed into the limo, "I've been thinking. From now on, you and I are gonna be equal partners, Daff. No more second banana for you."

Daffy smiled happily. "Thanks, pal. You know I —" Somebody slammed the limo door shut before he could finish his sentence.

". . . really appreciate it," he went on anyway. He watched the limo roll away. "Hey!" he cried. "Hey! Where's my entourage? Where are my assistants? What do *I* get?"

As if in answer, a huge light fell from the rigging high above Daffy, landing on him and flattening him into a duck pancake.

The camera panned over to another Daffy, lolling in a chair and sipping on a tropical drink. "Stunt duck," he explained with a wink.

Another light fell from the ceiling, flattening that Daffy, too.

Porky Pig thrust his face into the shot.

"Bibidi, bibidi, bibidi, that's all, folks!"